Babies in Rhinestones is Shena Mackay's first book for twelve years and her first collection of stories. She received wide acclaim for the five novels she wrote in her twenties, and has also written a screenplay for television and a play, *Nurse Macater*, for the National Theatre. She lives in Surrey.

Shena Mackay

BABIES IN RHINESTONES
and other stories

First published in Great Britain by
William Heinemann Ltd 1983
Published in Abacus by
Sphere Books Ltd 1984
30–32 Gray's Inn Road, London WC1X 8JL
Copyright © Shena Mackay, 1974, 1976, 1980, 1981, 1982, 1983

Publisher's Note

These stories are works of fiction. Names, characters, places and
incidents are either the product of the author's imagination or are used
fictitiously, and any resemblance to actual persons, living or dead,
events or locales is entirely coincidental.

Reproduced, printed and bound in Great Britain by
Hazell Watson & Viney Limited,
Aylesbury, Bucks

Contents

1 The Blue Orchestra   1
2 Bananas   13
3 Evening Surgery   23
4 Drying Out   53
5 Pink Cigarettes   71
6 Curry at the Laburnums   89
7 The Late Wasp   109
8 Family Service   127
9 Soft Volcano   141
10 The Stained-Glass Door   157
11 Babies in Rhinestones   169

For Sarah, Rebecca
and Cecily

Acknowledgements

'Soft Volcano' was first published in *New Review*, 1974.

'Curry at the Laburnums' was first published in *New Review*, 1976.

'The Stained-Glass Door' was first published in *Encounter Magazine*, 1981, and was read on BBC Radio 3, 1980.

'Bananas' was read on BBC Radio 3, 1982.

'Drying Out' was first published in *Quarto*, and read on BBC Radio 3, 1982.

'The Blue Orchestra' was first published in *Bindweed's Bestseller*, Pan Books Ltd, London, appeared in *Image Magazine*, and was read on BBC Radio 3, 1982.

The Blue Orchestra

The tropic day drew to its close, a full-blown rose falling into the half-melancholy sweetness of pot-pourri. On the verandah of the Hotel Miramar the Contessa Paloma and her consort, Oscar, gazed dreamily, over the opalescent sloosh of gin, the tiny sighs of lime and ice, across the bay; their intertwining fingers lay white and violet in her large and gauzy lap, while the blue orchestra conjured stars and fireflies out of the deepening sky; blue faces floated above blue instruments, blue fingers swept and plucked blue strings; while the island swayed to its rhythm, and the throb throb of the frogs from the swamp, in the mingled scents of musk and vanilla and the heavy white hiatus blossom.

The frogs' counterpoint grew louder, blurring the intricacies of the tune; the orchestra switched tempo to a wild tango, the blue instruments struggled, submerged and drowned in the clamour of croaks and shrieks and clashing wings of alarmed birds.

A silver figure loomed against the moon. The orchestra decamped. A violin shrieked in fear. A cocktail shaker exploded. The albino octoroon quartet, waiting in the wings to vocalise, melted like ice-cream. A creature

1

squelched towards the verandah uttering outlandish cries of 'Pam. Pam. Pam.'

The Contessa's habitual languor made her and Oscar the last to turn and flee after their fellow guests, the musicians and the waiter. The thing was upon them, falling to its knees, clutching the hem of the Contessa's dress.

'At last! It's taken me so long to find you!' – mangling the white material in its muddy hands. Oscar was pulling at the Contessa's hand.

'A revenant – Oh. The Undead. Oh. Run. Paloma,' he moaned.

'Get up!'

The Contessa rapped the revenant on the head with her parasol. It rose to reveal itself as a middle-aged woman streaked with silvery swamp mud, the wrecked nest of a frigate bird in a crazy garland round its neck.

'Run before she sucks your blood!' Oscar was gibbering desperately. 'Come on!'

'Calm yourself, my love. It's just some deranged person who has strayed into the swamp.'

'Don't you know me, Pam?'

A small frog leaped from her mouth.

'It's me, you twit, Sandy. Your best friend.' She shook the Contessa's sleeve. 'Sandra Sinclair that was. And is,' she admitted muddily.

'Take your hands off the Contessa Paloma!' commanded Oscar.

'Contessa Paloma my foot! That's old Pam Partridge!'

The Contessa swayed and might have fallen but for Oscar who helped her to a chair. The revenant plonked herself down beside her. Behind them the hotel staff crossed themselves from the safety of an upstairs window. Oscar was chafing the Contessa's wrists with gin.

'I don't know you. Why pick on me?'

'Because we are bloodbrothers, Pam.'

'No.'

'Don't you remember that night in the shrubbery when we pricked our fingers with my vice-hockey-captain's badge, and we mingled our blood and swore a solemn oath that we would always be true to one another?'

'I've never heard such nonsense in my life. I can only tell you that you must get back to the mainland at once. The monsoon will break any day now and the island will be marooned for weeks. The summer visitors have almost all gone – the last steamer leaves tonight – you could catch it if you ran.'

'Not likely! Not after coming all this way! If you knew what I've been through. . . .'

Even as she spoke a mournful hoot came from the jetty at the far end of the island.

The Contessa sank her head in her hands. A tendril of hair escaped and hung in a dark question mark on her white neck.

Oscar snapped his fingers for the waiter. No one came. He went into the hotel.

'I could murder a lager and lime!' called the revenant after him. 'And I wouldn't say no to a bag of crisps. Or a pie, or saveloy. Or even a ploughman's!'

'I must look a sight.' She ran her fingers through her hair and a shower of dried mud fell like wormcasts to the table. 'Lend us your bug-rake, Pam.'

'Bug-rake?' bleated the Contessa.

'Your comb!'

'No.' The Contessa clutched her bag. 'No. I haven't got one.'

The revenant's fantasies of food exploded in a dull burst of grease as Oscar returned empty-handed and trembling.

'We've been asked to leave,' he said incredulously. 'They won't serve us. They refuse to serve the Undead.' The Contessa gathered up her things.

'What *is* all this Undead stuff?' demanded the intruder.

'They live in the swamp. They are zombies, the living dead. They suck your blood, and if they do, you become one of them.'

'So the natives assume – ha ha – well, I assure you I'm very much alive and kicking.' She lashed out with a foot.

'To be thrown out of the Miramar!' Oscar repeated piteously. The Contessa supported him, a black tulip broken in a sudden storm, from the verandah.

'I've been barred from more pubs than you've had hot dinners,' the *soi-disant* Sandra Sinclair assured them cheerfully as she lolloped along beside them, shedding flakes of mud and exuding a rank smell of rotting lily stems.

'Where are we going?'

'Oscar and I are going home,' said the Contessa pointedly. 'So we must bid you goodnight.'

'Fair dos old girl. Bloodbrothers and all that!'

They arrived at the Villa Perroquet. 'I say, are you two shacked-up together? You sly old thing, Pam. Still, I can't say I'm surprised, looking back. Remember those coloured

4

workmen who came to mend the drains at school? Nudge, nudge. I'll never forget Mother Hubert's face when. . . .'

A passing bat drew a kindly veil over the rest of her sentence. Then she tottered in the doorway.

'I don't feel very well. Quick, where's the bog?'

Oscar sidestepped delicately.

'The bathroom,' said the Contessa, 'is through there. Next to it is the guest room, where, I suppose, you may sleep.'

In the morning, she thought grimly, she would get to the bottom of this bloodbrother nonsense. And squeeze the truth out of, or silence, Sandra Sinclair. Wasn't there something called a Chinese burn?

The Contessa lay veiled in mosquito nets, her scent evaporating in the night air.

'Oscar,' she called softly. 'Oscar.' At last she sighed and lit the lamp and picked at random from the pile on the bedside table a *Ladies' Home Journal* of July 1959, a relic of the brief occupation of the last missionary to visit the island.

'Can This Marriage Be Saved?' she read with a stab to the heart, but the page was so fretted by silverfish that it was little more than a doyley. She extinguished the lamp and lay, the Contessa Paloma or Pam Partridge, listening to the swish of the sea beyond the jalousies and was borne backwards on the tide and cast up on the shore of her dank girlhood. She had not lied when at first she denied all knowledge of Sandy Sinclair, but at the word hockey, memory like a bruise had suffused her brain. Now she was back in the art room of Belmont Towers, a small private school in Orpington, with a particularly unbecoming brown uniform, run by Anglican sisters. Beyond the window a seagull perched on a dead netball on the sleety hockey pitch, and inside, with chilblained fingers, she was dabbing blue powder-paint from a balding paint-brush onto sugar paper.

'A thoroughly silly piece of work. The perspective is all wrong. And an orchestra cannot be blue.' Sister Jerome had thrust her picture into the stove with a poker.

So many glass tiaras, aliases, false campaign ribbons, paste and pinchbeck baubles, forged cheques littered and glittered in the intervening years until she met and captured the heart of Oscar and sailed away with him, she had hoped forever, to the island where days were spent in dalliance and nights orchestrated by musicians whose blue instruments gave the lie to Sister Jerome, and whose heads and fingers were dyed indigo by the tropic dusk. And now Sandra Sinclair had come galumphing into Paradise out of the swamp to betray her. She saw a barren rhododendron, some blighted azaleas, but try as she might she could not dredge up any recollection of a ceremony in the shrubbery.

The Contessa woke early, pale and puffy-eyed, and stole out under the cover of unfamiliar snores to the bay, where lying on her back in the warm waves she was able to achieve for a few minutes the equanimity of a white porpoise.

'There were two Pamelas in our class. Pamela Peacock and Pamela Partridge,' she heard as she came up the steps. 'They were known as the two Pams.'

'Why?' came Oscar's voice.

The Contessa entered with her hair in a damp turban.

'Where's Eulogie?' she asked Oscar.

'It seems that she has deserted us. I've been trying to make coffee for ages,' he added plaintively, 'but the beans won't dissolve.'

'Darling, did you sleep in the hammock?' cried the Contessa tenderly. 'You're all criss-crossed like a string vest.'

He scowled and fiddled with his ear-ring. How she longed to cradle his cross head, the neat ears so closely set, the tiny chip of lapis lazuli glittering in one lobe.

Later as she sipped her bitter coffee she reflected on the defection of her little, her charming, her pretty little maid.

'Eulogie, of all people! It just goes to show you can't trust anyone.'

'Huh!'

Oscar leaped from the verandah and disappeared.

Sandy, evidently restored to health, was poking at the rind of a melon. 'Isn't there anything more substantial? One thing I learned in rep. was always to start the day with a decent breakfast – porridge, toast, bacon and egg.'

A small black pig ran squealing past and a guinea fowl flew into a tree as if in negation of her wish.

'Are you an actress then?'

'For my sins, as Mother Hubert would say. After you ran away the school put on a series of Morality plays and yours truly was cast in the lead. I caught the acting bug then and I've had the smell of grease-paint in my nostrils ever since! I've just been touring my one woman show in the States.'

'Aren't those Oscar's trousers? And his shirt?' interrupted the Contessa.

'I suppose so. I tried on a dress of yours and it just fell off me! I say, Pam, he's rather dishy, your Oscar, but isn't he – well – a little young for you?'

'How did you find me?'

Sandra Sinclair thrust her freckled knuckles into her eyes. 'You won't send me away, will you? I can't take any more, Pam. I've come to the end of the line. My tour was a disaster – I was booed from coast to coast – I had to pawn all my props and costumes – I was working my passage home when one day I saw you at the helm of a yacht. I knew you at once. I shouted and shouted, but you didn't hear me. I jumped overboard, but I couldn't swim fast enough. I managed to climb onto a dolphin's back, but it bit me. I was picked up by pirates – such brutes Pam, but so charming, too, they could be – I was forced to sail with them for months. Eventually they cast me adrift and I floated ashore. You can't imagine how I felt when I saw the self-same yacht I had seen you on lying on the beach – then I fell into the swamp. The rest you know.'

'That's all very well,' said the Contessa, 'but now, thanks to you, it is I who am likely to be cast adrift.' The dire warning, accompanied if necessary by a Chinese burn, which she was about to deliver died on her lips.

She caught sight of her erstwhile maid sneaking past with a bundle of her possessions which she had returned silently, through the kitchen door, to reclaim.

'Eulogie! Wait!'

The Contessa caught up with her. The girl smelled

8

faintly of trampled herbs from the kitchen garden, garlic and lemon balm.

'Dear, dear Eulogie, please don't go. She isn't a revenant, I promise. I swear.'

'That zombie goes, I come back.'

'I'm trying to get rid of her. She won't go. I don't want her here, I hate her!'

'That your hard cheddar.'

'But Eulogie, how shall we manage without you?'

Eulogie shrugged. 'It's her or me.'

'But she – she says she's my bloodbrother!'

Eulogie screamed and fled.

'Eu – log – eee. . . !'

Oscar lashed out miserably with a stick as he walked. He had spent a hideous night in the hammock. Some little children squatting by the roadside threading blossoms on a stem squealed and ran gibbering away. He threw a lime after them. It fell short and split in the dust. Like my heart, he thought. His eyes filled with tears. Lies. All lies. The false Contessa.

He passed an ancient shrine to the tortoise God, once the supreme deity of the islands – the mint and melon and cucumber floating in a votive glass of Pimm's set on the worn stone were already looking limp, the wreath of melon flowers wilting and jaded – the island had been converted to Christianity in 1857, but there were still irregular outbreaks of tortoise worship in the remoter parts.

At the sound of a bell he looked up at the monastery, set

on the highest pinnacle of the island, home of the monks of St Onan, an enclosed order rarely seen outside its walls, where the blind old Abbot, guided by a boy, was leading the purple-robed brothers to the chapel. Oscar wondered if he should apply for a novitiate. He skirted the swamp, crossing himself, and found himself at the bay where his little motor yacht, *The Faithful Dove*, rode prettily at anchor on the green waves. Perhaps he should rename her 'The Perfidious Partridge'. He gazed for some minutes at the distant opal, shimmering in the haze, that was his native island, then pitched a pebble at the boat's white bows, and his tears fell into the silver sand as he walked back up the beach to the Villa Perroquet.

'What do you two do with yourselves all day?' Sandra demanded during their silent and exiguous lunch – the Contessa had felt strong enough only to open a tin of Dead Sea fruit. 'Well, what do you do in the evenings then?' she persisted.

'We used to go to the Miramar,' replied Oscar heavily, refilling his glass and taking it onto the verandah. Sandy followed him.

'Such exotic blooms,' she murmured. 'What's this flower called?'

'Noli me tangere.'

'That's Latin isn't it? Ouch!'

'I say, Pam,' she said to the Contessa who had emerged hopefully at the sound of her shriek, 'do you remember that time when you crept into Sister Anselm's room with a bottle of red ink and in the morning she thought she had received the Stigmata? That was a real hoot!'

'No.'

'We had respect for the Sisters who taught us,' said Oscar, visibly shocked. 'They beat us with palm fronds for the slightest misdemeanour.'

Sandy gazed doubtfully at the droopy leaves susurrating softly in the breeze.

'It was the principle of the thing.'

'Oh well, Sister Jerome . . .,' she began, but her friend lashed her with her eyes.

'Would you like me to do a comic monologue?' offered Sandy that evening.

Oscar appeared to be asleep. The Contessa did not look up from her jigsaw which depicted a map of England.

'Damn,' she said. 'Surrey's missing. Oh well, I never did feel at home in the Home Counties.'

'Don't ever mention the Dorking Halls to me!' Sandy shuddered at the memory of some fiasco. Neither of them should have thought of doing so.

'You told me you were educated in a convent outside Bilbao,' Oscar spoke to the Contessa for the first time that day. His speech was slightly slurred.

'Si Señor,' she countered, flourishing an invisible castanet. 'That was – *plus tard.*' She laughed gaily, grinding her teeth.

'Huh.'

'Don't grimace like that, darling,' she begged. 'The wind might change.'

'It has,' he said. 'They're putting up the shutters at the Miramar.'

Sandy could not sleep. She thrashed like a netted fish under her mosquito net, listening to an uneasy wind lifting the jalousies and dropping them again. Something was troubling her, nibbling like a silverfish at the edge of her brain. Then she stifled a scream. It was Pam Peacock not Pam Partridge she had met in the shrubbery, mingled her blood with and sworn eternal friendship to. She lay prickled by cold sweat in the sweltering bed with the dreadful realisation throbbing in her brain. Then she clamped her pillow firmly over her head to suffocate it.

The Contessa woke from such a pleasant and vivid dream of sailing round the bay that she could still hear the chug chug of the boat's engine as she lay in the darkness. Suddenly she sat upright in bed.

'Oscar,' she shouted, 'Oscar, she's gone! She's taken the boat!' The sound of the motor was lost in the swell of the sea. An explosion of thunder shook the villa, the wind wrenched off the shutters and flung great drops of rain at the windows. A blue flash of lightning blazed for a second like magnesium, then in the black aftermath the Contessa felt the side of the bed sag.

'Darling,' she cried holding out her arms.

'Budge up, Pam,' said a little girlish voice. 'I'm scared!'

Bananas

'Gin? You want cheap gin?'

In vain had she oiled her basket on wheels. The dreadful young man leaped from his doorway and was standing on the opposite pavement shouting at her.

Imogen Lemon's face swelled into one of the gross, foreign, beefsteak tomatoes sunning themselves outside his shop and such a headache hit her brow that she felt her skin would split and spill hot seeds onto her white sundress. She hurried to the safety of the supermarket, thirsting for one of the discreet little English tomatoes that had graced the shop before it fell into the hirsute hands of its present owner. The wicker basket followed at her heels like a faithful stiff old Airedale.

Two tiny veiled women in black passed in a cloud of patchouli. Imogen Lemon was a tall, slender divorcée with long hands and feet which had been much admired. Once her boss, coming upon her unexpectedly, typing in the gloaming, had momentarily mistaken her for a young girl seated at the virginals. Now she felt suddenly huge and white and freakish and half-naked in her summer frock against these scented bolts of black silk, and resented it.

On these warm evenings, after her supper and the nine o'clock news, Imogen would pour a tiny amount of gin into a tall glass and carry it, with slimline tonic brimming big rocks of ice, onto her balcony where she smoked two slow cigarettes and read the paper, the noise of the traffic blurred by the darkening leaves, and would sit in her iron garden in the sky until the leaves were black and the roses white and the glass an insubstantial rind floating at her foot.

Now, with him shouting out to the street like that about cheap gin, she felt as though his prickly face had thrust through the perfumed air, dirtying the roses.

She should never have bought gin in his shop.

The trouble was, she reflected gloomily as she trailed round the supermarket, his shop was so handy. She would often pop in after work for something quick for supper or, when Claud, her cat, declared that his breakfast smelled and was unfit for feline consumption, she could dash through the traffic for a packet of frozen fish and be back in five minutes. Lately, however, the young man's stock seemed to have deteriorated. Of course it was not his fault that they were demolishing the buildings opposite and brick dust drifted through the open door and settled in a reddish haze on everything, although she supposed that he could employ one of his mothy feather dusters to remove it, instead of lounging about exchanging gibberish with his cronies in the back of the shop. And, of course, if she should need a card of rusty hair grips or a dented tin of chick peas, a pair of tights with one leg shorter than the other, or a tub of gangrenous yogurt at midnight, a Christmas pudding in July or Easter eggs at Christmas, it was nice to know that he was there.

She would not touch his meat, however; and always avoided looking at the strange red glossy animals, peeled heads and foreshortened limbs that hinted at barbarism under their sweaty perspex cover. She left the supermarket and went into the butcher's, shouldering the English beasts of honest yeoman stock that hung in the doorway.

As she emerged, a troupe of goblins flurried round her, banging her knees, and one trod heavily on her toe. As she gasped and disengaged herself, clutching at the wall with one hand and her spinning basket on wheels with the other, she realised it was only the little girls from the preparatory school, in their distinctive red caps and lethal sandals, on their way to the swimming baths. She limped home.

That evening a storm broke on West Kensington and Imogen was quite pleased to give in to her headache and sore toe and retire early, conjuring up, as usual, an angel, in a long white nightdress not dissimilar to her own, at each corner of her bed.

In the morning, as she passed on her way to the tube, he was outside the shop unpacking a crate of bananas. He straightened and stood grinning at her through the very small white pointed teeth that glittered in his stubbly muzzle. The sun struck a gold medallion lying in the black curls that gushed from his chest and eddied round his throat, and turned the stiff fans of hair at the armholes of his blue singlet to a rusty coral. He thrust a bunch of bananas in her face.

'You want bananas? Very good today.'

'No, thank you . I'm on my way to work. Perhaps later.'

She forgot about him but on her way home she saw him, from the corner of her eye, on the other side of the road waving a banana at her. She steadfastly, if painfully walked on. She did not know his name, so Bananas was what she came to call him to herself.

Later that evening she slipped out in sunglasses and plastic mac to the Victoria Wine for a bottle of tonic. Her toe was still swollen, so as well as enjoying the comfort of them, she felt that her pink slippers added the finishing touch to her disguise. On her return Claud leaped at her as if congratulating her on her cunning, and she was laughing into his fur when the telephone rang.

'Mum?'

'Hello, Jenny darling.'

'You sound very cheerful.'

'Yes, well. . . .'

'We thought we might come to see you on Sunday. . . .'

As she shook hands with Father Smillie on the church path and shook the scent of incense and a drifting lime flower from her hair, it came to Imogen that she should buy some limes for their pre-luncheon drinks. Fortified by the rites of the Holy Church, she decided to brave Bananas. By a small miracle he was in the back of the shop with a chum and an exquisite little boy in a long white nightshirt was standing by the fruit display outside.

'Two limes, please.'

What a tragedy that Time would turn him into another Bananas. . . .

He reached for two greenish warty lemons.

'No, dear. I said limes. Those are lemons,' she told him firmly.

'Two limes.'

'No. Those are lemons. I asked for limes,' she said very slowly and clearly. 'Those small green things are limes. Could you give me two, please, I'm in rather a hurry?'

She was about to reach for them herself when Bananas hurtled into the doorway, snatched the lemons from the boy, dropped them into a paper bag and handed them to her.

'No! I don't want them. I want limes!'

'You don't want?'

'I want two limes!'

'Ah!'

He reached up, took two limes and dropped them into the bag.

'Seventy-four pence. Anything else for you today? Bananas, gin, cigarettes?'

Half-blinded and deafened by a wash of tears, she saw his little teeth moving as she put down the money and, blundering through the door, collided with a woman in black, whose beaked mask gave her cheek a sharp peck.

'You see, I was beginning to think the whole thing was an elaborate joke at my expense. An absurd pun on my name. That he had somehow found out my name – silly,

17

really. . . .' Her voice trailed off. Obviously they found her story completely incomprehensible.

They were sitting on the balcony, the slices of lime stranded on melted ice in the bottoms of their glasses, Imogen, Jennifer and her husband Tony and Toby the baby who had a clownish red circle on each cheek and who was grizzling and banging his head on his mother's chest.

'You mean this woman deliberately attacked you with her beak?' asked Jennifer, warding off another blow from the hard head.

'No, of course not. Shall we go in and eat?'

'I'm awfully sorry, Mum,' Jennifer said as she surveyed the goodies spread out on the table, 'Toby won't eat anything when he's teething. Could he just have a banana?'

'A banana?' Imogen looked desperately at the blue grapes and oranges in the fruit bowl. 'I suppose I could pop across the road. . . .'

'I'd go, only he screams if I put him down.'

Imogen looked at Tony, but he had buried his face in *The Sunday Times*. No hope there.

The baby flung out a fist and pointed at the door.

'Of course,' Imogen said weakly, picking up her purse.

Two elderly men in white robes with red and white checked tea-towels on their heads pushed past her as she went into the shop with her bunch of bananas, got into a limousine parked outside, and were driven away. She joined the queue at the checkout and a black robe fell in behind her. Bananas seemed gloomy, even morose, she was pleased to notice. Perhaps his visitors had upset him. He grabbed the bananas and bashed them, bruisingly, into the scales.

'You got no need to go to Victoria Wine for gin,' he accused her, 'I got cheap gin. You want any today? Any cigarettes?'

To her horror she saw that it was not a black-robed woman behind her, but Father Smillie in his soutane. And Bananas was waving a bottle of gin.

The luncheon party was not a success. The children left early, using Toby's teeth as an excuse, and Imogen was left trying to drown Bananas' voice in the washing-up water, but Father Smillie wouldn't go down the drain.

On the following Sunday she was too ashamed to face him at Mass and had to take a bus to the Brompton Oratory. When she returned she saw the limousine parked again outside the shop and the sound of angry voices came across the road.

She had resolved never to enter his shop again and to ignore him if he spoke to her, but several days later Bananas caught her as she passed with her basket on wheels.

'Good morning. What can I get you today?'

'Nothing, thank you. I'm on my way to the library,' she lied.

'You like books. I got lots of books.'

Imogen looked past him, at his dubious stock of literature.

19

'I only read the classics,' she lied again.

'I got classics. You want *Lady Chatterley*, *The Thorn Birds*, *Third Term at Malory Towers?*'

Thus it happened that she was standing, a lurid-covered paperback in her hand, and Bananas calling from within, 'Any gin today?', as Father Smillie passed her with a curt nod, his soutane freaked with brick dust, hurrying from some errand of mercy on the demolition site.

'Cheap gin and cigarettes. Cheap gin and cigarettes,' the little girls were chanting as they skipped in the playground as she passed. Imogen tried to convince herself that they were saying something quite different, but that did it. She arranged to take a week of her holiday at once, organised a neighbour to look after Claud, and fled to a friend's cottage in Ilfracombe.

As she lay on the beach, healed by the waves and sand, she saw how absurd the whole thing had become.

On her return she strode on tanned legs into the shop to buy some special fish as a homecoming present for Claud, determined to restore Bananas to his right proportions – a foolish, over-friendly, small, foreign shopkeeper who must be politely but firmly shown his place.

A strange man, trim of beard and neat of collar and tie, stood behind the till.

'The other man, the one who used to be here, is he away?' she asked.

'He's gone.'

'Gone? Isn't he coming back?'

'No.'

'Why not?'

'He was losing money. He bad man. He won't be back.'

'Oh.'

Imogen felt a strange disappointment as she turned away. 'Oh,' she said again and her eye for once lingered on the meat display where a fly sat up on the perspex lid and rubbed its hands. Between two writhing heaps of mince was the boiled head of some animal, and set in its glistening jaws were two rows of tiny, very white, pointed teeth.

Evening Surgery

A Chopin prelude was strained through the speaker that stood on a little shelf on the surgery wall above a garish oil painting that shone in the cruel neon striplight that picked out the lines and blemishes and red-hawed eyes of the patients on the black vinyl benches. Mavis Blizzard, senior receptionist, was proud of that picture; it had been painted by one of 'her' old ladies, a purblind resident of Peacehaven House for the Elderly, which she visited regularly, cheering up the old girls, surreptitiously putting right the great holes and loops that shaky fingers made in bits of knitting, jollying them along when they grew tearful over old snap-shots that she had persuaded them to show. No matter that the picture was upside down, the artist had now lost her sight completely; it would hang as a testament to their friendship. From time to time the name of one of the four doctors flashed on a board, a buzzer sounded and a patient departed; the telephone rang, Mavis answered it, and greeted favoured customers by name when they came through the door; her two minions busied themselves among files and coffee cups; although they wore blue

23

overalls like Mavis's own, they seemed interchangeable, merged into one subdued lady in glasses, for she was the star of the surgery. Sounds of passing cars came through the glittering black panes of the window, people coughed, pages turned. The music stopped abruptly, then an orchestral selection from *South Pacific* washed softly over the surgery.

'That's better!' announced Mavis Blizzard brightly. 'We'd all have been asleep in a minute. Dr Frazer's choice. Much too highbrow for my taste.'

She was leaning out of the hatch behind which she operated and enveloped her audience in a conspiratorial wink. As she opened her eye she couldn't believe that the young woman in the corner was almost glaring at her. She had a quick read of her notes before sending them into Doctor. An invisible hand had placed a cup of coffee at her elbow; she clattered the pink cup with a red waxy smear on its rim onto the saucer.

'Well, I won't be sorry to get home tonight. I've been on my feet since six o'clock this morning and my poor hubby will have to get his own tea tonight. It's his Church Lads' Band night. They're practising some carols to entertain the old folks at my senior citizens' party, bless them,' she announced to one of her sidekicks or to the surgery at large.

If there were any who thought that her husband had had a lucky reprieve, they were rifling through the *Reader's Digest* or *Woman and Home* and registered nothing.

The telephone rang.

'Hello, you're through to surgery appointments.'

Her voice grew louder.

'Of course, Mr Jackson. Is it urgent, only Doctor's very booked up tomorrow? What seems to be the trouble? Pardon? Oh, your waterworks, Mr Jackson.'

Someone sniggered behind the *Tatler*, others squirmed on the squeaky vinyl at this public shaming. It was enough to send two girls into fits; they snorted through their noses. The old man beside them moved an inch or two away from their cropped, hennaed heads, their ear-rings, their dark red mouths.

'You'll be old yourselves someday and it won't seem so funny then,' he said. The comic they hid behind shook in disbelief. Mavis Blizzard rolled her eyes; her own daughter was a Queen's Guide.

' – well,' she went on, 'Doctor's got a late surgery on Thursday. We could squeeze you in then at eleven forty-five. That's eleven forty-five on Thursday then. Not at all. See you Thursday then. Byee, – by which time the unfortunate man might be damned or drowned.

'Deaf as a post, bless him,' she explained.

'Next Patient for Dr Frazer' flashed up on the board. The woman in the corner jumped up, tossing her magazine onto the table, upsetting the neat pile. Mavis watched her disappearing jeans disapprovingly. She prided herself on getting on with all sorts, you had to in this job, but this one she definitely did not trust.

The woman walked into the consulting room. The doctor rose.

'Cathy! How've you been?'

'Bloody awful. You?'

'The same.'

She sat down. He took her hand across the desk.

'It's good to see you.'

'Yes.'

She was staring at the desk, twisting a paperclip with her other hand. There was so much to say, and nothing. They sat in silence. Then, as if suddenly aware of the briefness of their time together, he came round to her side of the desk.

When Mrs Blizzard had to come in to fetch a file the patient was buttoning her shirt. Dr Frazer stood beside her. Nothing unusual about that. So why did she feel as if she was fighting her way through an electric storm? The stethoscope lay on the desk.

'Come and see me again if the pain persists,' said Dr Frazer.

'OK,' she replied casually, without so much as a thank you or goodbye. Mavis rolled her eyes at the doctor, expecting a confirmatory twinkle at this rudeness, but he was grinning like a fool at the closing door.

'Well, really!' she said.

He pressed the buzzer as she went out. Nobody appeared. He was just going to buzz again when Mavis led in a frail old lady and helped her onto the chair.

'Let's make you comfy. I'll just pop this cushion behind your back.'

What a kind soul she is, the doctor thought. He realised that he hated her.

'Well, Miss Weatherby, let's have a look at you.' What's left of you, he almost said.

She struck the cushion to the floor with a tiny, surprisingly strong, gloved hand.

'I want you to give me a certificate, Doctor.'

'What kind of certificate?'

'A certificate to confirm that I am unfit; not well enough to attend her senior citizens' party!'

He had to fumble in his desk drawer, but she had seen his face.

'You can laugh, you don't have to go!'

She was laughing too, but tears glittered in her eyes.

'Neither do you, surely?'

'She's threatening to collect me in her car. I'll have to wear a paper hat and sing carols to the accompaniment of her husband's appalling boys' band, and then her daughter will hide behind the door and shake a bell and she will say, "Hark! What's that I hear? Can it be sleighbells?" and her husband will leap into the room in a red plastic suit and give us bathcubes '

'Couldn't you pretend a prior engagement?'

'She's managed to ferret out that I have no family or friends. She wants me to move into Peacehaven as soon as there's a coffin, I mean a bed.'

'I'm afraid I can't really give you a certificate, but I'll have a word if you like, about the party . . .', wondering how he could.

'It wouldn't do any good. I'll just have to turn out the lights and lie in bed until she's gone.'

'No you won't. Come and spend the evening with us. I

27

can't promise any paper hats or bathcubes, but it would be nice if you did. OK?'

'OK,' she managed.

As she left he saw that her legs had shrunk to two sticks around which her stockings hung like pale, deflated balloons. Time unravels us, he thought, like old, colourless silk flags in churches, which have outlasted their cause.

At home, Mary's eyes, which lately a vague unhappiness had turned a darker blue, dimmed and were brighter, like mussels washed by a little wave, when he told her of Miss Weatherby's plight.

'Of course she must come. But why does she hate Mavis? She's so kind.'

'She's a ghoul. She feeds on illness and disease and death!' he burst out.

'But. . . .' Mary closed her mouth. She went to the sideboard and poured him a drink, as she gave it to him he took her hand and kissed it. 'Thank you,' he said.

When Catherine opened the gate of the little terraced house she shared with her daughter and son she saw the room as a stranger might, through the unpulled curtains, lit from within like a candle whose wick has burned down below its rim; the paper moon suspended from the ceiling, the bowl of satsumas, the old chairs, the television glowing softly like a tank of tropical fish; the familiar tenderised and made strange by the darkness.

At seven o'clock in the morning a soapy fragment of

moon was dissolving in the damp sky; birds assembled in the trees to wait for their breakfast, black shapes against the blue that slowly suffused the cloud; Catherine sat on the back step. She was glad that he could not see her in the old summer dress she was wearing as a nightdress, Lucy's clogs and her ex-husband's ropey bathrobe; her eyes stung as she looked along the length of her cigarette, such a lot to get through, her mouth felt thick and dry; behind her in the kitchen the washing machine threw a last convulsion and gave a little sob, like a child who has fallen asleep crying. Paul would be back from his paper round in a minute. She went in and ran a bath. As she lay in the water, left disagreeably tepid by the washing machine's excesses, she saw how she had failed with her husband, whose robe huddled in a heap on the floor; she had never let him see that she needed him. Because she had known that he would fail her. But if she had. She recalled Hardy's poem 'Had you but wept'. Such watery half-thoughts as float past when people are alone and naked vanished with the bubbles down the plughole.

She put the kettle on, switched on the radio, woke Lucy, made tea, made toast, made two packed lunches, flung the washing over the line, a jumble of socks and jeans and shirts that would not dry in the damp air, tested Lucy on her Latin while she combed her hair and coaxed some moribund mascara onto her lashes; the phone rang – for Lucy; wrote a note for Paul who had been absent the day before; the phone rang again; Paul, eating the remains of yesterday's pudding from the fridge, dropped the bowl on the floor, Lucy ironed a PE shirt and the pop music on the radio crackled like an electric drill so she turned it up. No doubt, Catherine thought sourly, the Frazers are sitting down to muesli and motets. Someone called; the children left.

She found a splinter of glass on the floor near the sink and held it up to the light from the window. If one just stared at pretty glass fragments or soap bubbles or the sediment round the taps or studied the patterns left by spilled pudding on the tiles. Is that what it's like to be mad; or sane? But if everyone did there would be no glass, no iridescent bubbles in the washing-up bowl. Even as these thoughts drifted through her mind the glass splinter was in the pedal bin, a cloth was attacking the bleary taps. As she attempted to leave the house a plant pulled her back with a pale parched reproachful frond. 'I'll water you tonight,' she promised, but had to run back for the watering can and then run down the road, as usual, to the bookshop where she worked.

Her legs ached. With every book token, every cookery book, every DIY handbook, every copy of *Old Surrey in Pictures*, *Bygone Surrey*, *Views of Old Guildford*, *Views of Old Reigate*, *Views of Old Dorking*, every *Wine Bibber's Guide* that she sold she felt less Christmassy. How stupid and greedy the customers were, flapping cheque books at her and Pat, the other assistant, slapping fivers down on the counter so that they had to pick them up, taking all the change so that she had to go to the bank twice for more.

'Isn't Christmas shopping murder? Isn't it Hell?' the customers said. 'I'll be glad when it's all over!'

Greetings flew from throats that sounded as if they were already engorged with mincemeat. No doubt several books were slipped into shopping bags.

'It must be lovely working here – all these lovely books!' people told them. 'I could browse for hours!'

'Oh, yes!' Pat agreed mistily, not seeing the floor which muddy feet had reduced to a football pitch and which she would not clean. She was twenty-nine and wore little girl shoes, and dresses which she made herself; Cathy thought that she must be too embarrassed to take her own measurements, because they never fitted very well. She spent her lunch hours in the stockroom eating packets of pale meat sandwiches and drinking tisanes, reading childrens' books and lives of the saints. Mr Hermitage, the shop's owner, who was bowing and gesticulating like a puppet in his velvet suit in the back of the shop, and who was too mean to employ a cleaner, did not like to ask Pat to wash the floor so Catherine's less spiritual hands were calloused by the mop.

When she got the chance Catherine went into the little kitchen behind the stockroom and put on the kettle and lit a cigarette. There was nowhere to sit so she leaned on the sink.

'I won't go to the surgery tonight,' she told herself 'I mustn't. I know it's wrong. It's stealing. I'm not going to go.'

Mr Hermitage came in rubbing his hands.

'Coffee! That's good!'

His body contrived to brush against hers, as it always did.

'Sorry,' he said, patting her as if it had been an accident, as he always did.

She carried her coffee and a cup of cowslip tea for Pat into the shop, taking a gulp on the way to drown the smell of nicotine. Six or seven people stood at the counter, impatient at the speed of the two robots behind it. Pat rolled panic-stricken eyes at her; she was up to her ankles in spoiled wrapping paper. The sellotape sneered and snarled. As Catherine reached into the till Pat pressed the cash total button and the drawer slammed on her fingers. She yelled and swore. The customers looked offended; shop assistants' fingers don't have feelings, especially at Christmas time. Catherine waited for her nails to turn black. Now she would have to go to the surgery. Alas, her fingers remained red and painful, but could not justify medical treatment. Her hopes abated with the swelling.

She arrived home late that evening and dumped her heavy carrier bag. It had taken ages to do the money; it had been twelve pounds short. Pat had been flustered into making several over-rings; customers had asked for books and then changed their minds after they had been rung up, there was an unsigned cheque. Catherine's face ached with smiling at browsers and buyers; she had eaten nothing all day. There was a warm smell of cooking.

'Dinner's almost ready,' said Lucy.

'I've made you a cup of tea, Mum,' said Paul.

She did not let herself notice the potato peelings in the sink, the spilled sugar, the teabag on the floor, which he had thrown at the pedal bin, and missed, the muddy rugby boots on the draining board.

32

'You're dear, kind children,' she said. She unbent her cold fingers one by one.

'Mum? . . . Are you all right? I mean, you're not ill or anything are you?'

'Of course I'm not. Why?'

'It's just that you look so sad. You never smile. And you went to the doctor's.'

'It's just the Christmas rush in the shop. You've no idea what hell it is.'

Catherine felt ashamed. She saw that she was dragging them into into her own abyss.

'Nobody's going out tonight, are they? And nobody's coming round? Good.'

She wanted to draw them to her, to spend the sort of family evening they had enjoyed before this madness had overtaken her; the curtains closed, the gas fire blooming like a bed of lupins, the telly on; the sort of evening you thought nothing of.

Halfway through 'Top of the Pops' the phone rang.

'I'll get it!' Catherine grabbed the receiver with crossed fingers.

'Hello, could I speak to Lucy, please?'

Dumbly she handed it over. They had agreed that he should not ring or come to the house. And yet. . . .

Later the doorbell rang; Catherine clamped herself to her chair.

'Door, Paul.'

A male voice at the door. She stopped herself from running to the mirror and glued her eyes to her book, looking up slowly as Paul slouched back, behind him John

33

Frazer metamorphosed into a tall boy, through a sort of grey drizzle.

'Hi. I've come to copy Paul's maths.'

'Oh. How about some coffee, Paul?' Or a quadruple gin. Or a cup of hemlock.

As the boys went to the kitchen Catherine said to Lucy, 'Actually I don't feel very well. I keep getting headaches. The doctor gave me something for them, but it doesn't seem to work. I think I'd better go back tomorrow . . . so don't worry if I'm a bit late. . . . Well, I suppose I'd better get on with the ironing.'

'Would you like me to do it?'

'Of course, but I'd rather you did your homework.'

Anyway it would kill an hour or so.

The case of a certain Dr Randal and a Mrs Peacock had, naturally, aroused much interest among the receptionists in the surgery. Mr Peacock had brought an action against the doctor, accusing him of the seduction of his wife and it had become a minor *cause célèbre*, partly because there were those who thought that the rules should be changed, partly because there had been no meaty scandal of late, no politicians floundering in the soup. Dressed like their namesakes, he in flashy tie and cufflinks, she in drab brown tweed plumage, an invisible blanket of shame over her bowed head, the Peacocks strutted and scurried across evening television screens and stared greyly from the newspaper in Mavis Blizzard's hand.

'Of course, it's the woman I blame in a case like this; a

doctor's in such a vunerable position. . . . It's the children I feel sorry for. And his poor wife! What she must be going through.'

Mrs Peacock must be pecked to pieces by the rest of the flock; her brown feathers, torn by Mavis's sharp bill, drifted about the surgery.

'And she's not even pretty!'

'Must have hidden charms,' came with a timid snort from behind Mavis.

'Ssh.'

If their words were not, as she suspected, directed at Catherine, they none the less pierced the magazine she was using as a shield and managed to wound.

Mavis slotted in a cassette of Christmas carols and hummed along with it. A sickly fragrance of bathcubes emenated from her sanctum; she was wrapping them for her senior citizens' party, in between answering the phone and all her other tasks. Her daughter, Julie, who had come in to give her a hand, nudged her.

'That's Paul Richards's mother. He goes to our school. He's really horrible. This afternoon he and his friends turned on all the taps in the cloakroom and flooded it. They were having a fight with the paper towels. You never saw such a mess! Water all over the place, other people's belongings getting soaked! I wouldn't like to be them tomorrow morning!' she concluded with satisfaction.

A little boy, about two years old, was running round the table, bumping into people's knees, falling over their feet. His mother grew tired of apologising and held him captive. He screamed and would not be pacified. She had to let him go.

'What's all this then? What's all the noise about?'

Mavis Blizzard had emerged and was advancing in a sort of crouch in her blue overall on the startled child who backed into his mother's knees.

'We can't have you disturbing all my ladies and gentlemen, can we? Let's see if I've got anything in my pockets for good little boys, shall we?'

He clenched his hands behind his back. Mavis winked at his mother and dangled a sweet. The child gave a sob and flung himself on his mother banging his hard, hot head on her lip. A red weal sprang up immediately and the glassy eyes spilled over. The child joined a loud grizzling to her silent tears.

'I think we'd better let this little fellow see Doctor next, don't you?' Mavis looked round, 'That is, if nobody objects?'

Nobody objected. The mother jerked to her feet a silent girl in glasses who had kept her head bent over a comic throughout, and ran the gauntlet with her and the crying boy and a heavy shopping bag.

'Poor kid,' remarked Mavis as she returned to her hatch. 'She does find it hard to cope, bless her. My heart bleeds for these one-parent families. Not that I'm one to make judgements, live and let live, and lend a helping hand where you can, that's my motto.'

For a moment they were all bathed in her tolerance.

'Drat that phone! Blessed thing never stops, does it?' Evidently she forgot that most of her audience had been guilty. . . .

'Hello, you're through to the surgery, can I help you? Of course. I'll drop the prescription in myself on my way home. No, it's no trouble at all. Save you turning out on your poor old legs in this nasty weather. No, it's hardly out of my way at all, and I shall be late home anyway. We've got a full house tonight!' She uttered the noise which served her for a laugh.

Catherine looked at her watch; the appointments were running ten minutes late. She reached for another magazine and saw a jar of carnations on the windowsill, slender stems in the beaded water, like cranes' green delicate legs. As the bubbles streamed to the surface and clustered round the birds' knees she wished she had not come; she wished she was at home cooking the evening meal. It was absurd; it was making neither of them happy.

'You said to come back if the pain persists. It persists.'

'Thank you for coming tonight. I've missed you so much.'

To her dismay she was crying. He scorned the box of pink tissues provided by Mavis for patients who wept and gave her his own white handkerchief. Even as she dried her eyes she realised that it had been laundered by his wife; it didn't help.

'It's not enough,' she said. 'At first it was enough just to know that you were on the same planet. Then I thought, if only we could be alone for five minutes, then it was an hour, then an evening . . . it's almost worse than nothing.'

The door handle squeaked. Instinctively she leaped from his arms to the couch and turned her face to the wall as Mavis came in.

'Mrs Blizzard! I wish you wouldn't barge in when I'm with a patient!'

'You forget that I'm a trained nurse,' she bridled. 'Dr MacBeth always asks me to be present when he's examining a female patient. I'm sorry to have disturbed you!'

She slammed the door behind her.

'I know it's not enough,' he said quickly. 'Can you get out one evening? Meet me somewhere?'

'Yes.' So that was that. How easily principles, resolutions not to hurt anybody died.

He leaned over the couch and kissed her; she felt the silky hair on the back of his neck, his ear; she felt his hand run gently down her body, on her thigh.

'Don't, don't,' she said, but she didn't take his hand away.

'An urgent call for you, Dr Frazer,' squawked Mavis through the intercom.

Catherine slid off the couch and found the floor with trembling legs. Her face was burning.

'Just a minute,' he put his hand over the receiver. 'I love you. See you tomorrow morning? About eleven? We'll arrange something.'

Outside in the street she found his handkerchief in her hand and buried her face in it and looking up, saw the stars over its white edge. As she lay in bed that night she put her hand where his hand had been.

He was late. She pushed her trolley up and down the aisles of Safeways, putting in something from time to time for appearance's sake, waiting, loitering, buffeted, causing obstructions.

'I'm sorry.'

She whirled round. The smile withered on her face. A little girl was seated in his trolley. He rolled his eyes towards his wife's back, at the deli. counter. As Mary turned to them he said, 'How are you?'

'As well as can be expected.'

She blundered to the checkout with her almost empty trolley.

'. . . a patient,' she heard him explain, betray.

After crying for a while in the precinct she had to go to Sainsburys to finish her shopping and trudge home to transform herself from lovesick fool into mother. Loud music hit her as she opened the front door. An open biscuit tin stood on the kitchen table, seven or eight coffee cups had been placed thoughtfully in the sink; she had to wash them before she could start on the potatoes. Several pairs of muddy shoes lay about the floor. Teenage laughter came from the bedrooms. Not jealousy. Not bitterness. Just pain. Like the dull knife blade stabbing a potato. The telephone rang. Feet thudded towards it.

'She's not in.'

'I am in!' She shouted and ran to the telephone.

'Cathy?' Her ex-husband.

'Oh, it's you.'

She had to stop herself from hurling the receiver at the wall.

'Cathy, I was wondering about Christmas. . . .'

'Yes?'

'Well, I just . . . I mean, what are you doing?'

'Oh, this and that. One or two parties. The children have lots of things on. We're going to my parents' on Boxing Day, all the family will be there. I suppose we'll go to church on Christmas Day. Why?'

She longed to be beyond the tinsel and crackers, in the greyness of January where melancholy was the norm.

'Well, I just wondered. I mean, it's a bit of a bleak prospect – the kids and all. . . .'

'You mean you want to come here. You may as well. It makes no difference to me. Why not? It will make every-thing just about perfect.'

She replaced the receiver, not wanting to wonder about whatever desperation had driven him to call, unable to contemplate any pain but her own.

At last the three of them sat down to lunch.

'Mum?'

'What?'

'We are going to get a tree, aren't we?'

She looked at her children, her babies; Lucy's long hair glittering in the electric light, Paul's pretty spikes. She determined to stop being such a pain.

'Of course we are. We always do, don't we? I thought we might go this afternoon.'

'Great.'

'You'll come, won't you, Paul?'

'Well, you'll need me to carry it, if we get a big one, won't you?'

At nine o'clock that night John was called to Miss Weatherby's house. A neighbour, taking his dog for a

40

stroll, had been alarmed by her milk-bottle on the step, her newspaper jutting from the door, and had found the old lady very ill. Had she had any family, John might have comforted them: she died in my arms; but she had none. He drove away feeling infinitely sad. There was only one person he wanted to tell about it; to lie in her arms and be comforted, to have wiped away the memory of the one card on Miss Weatherby's mantelpiece which said, 'A Merry Xmas From Your Unigate Milkman'. He stopped at an off-licence and bought a bottle of whisky. What a shabby figure he had cut, with furtive meetings in the surgery and Safeways. Why hadn't he telephoned her this morning after the fiasco in Safeways? OK, so he hadn't been alone for a minute, but he could have made some excuse to get out to a call-box, couldn't he? Why on earth did she put up with him? There could be only one reason. She loved him. He switched on the radio. Music flooded the car. He was singing as he drove into her road. Soft pink and green and yellow stars, Christmas tree lights, glowed against black windows. He was touched by these talismans in little human habitations. But when he reached her house he couldn't park. A line of cars stretched along each side of the street. He caught the poignant sparkle of her Christmas tree in a gap in the curtains. He found a space in the next road and walked back. The terraced house seemed to be jumping up and down between its neighbours, blazing with loud music. A volley of laughter hit him. He turned and walked away. He dumped the bottle in its fragile tissue paper in a litter-bin.

As Catherine cleared away the remains of last night's

impromptu party from the carpet the telephone rang faintly through the hoover's noise. She switched off. Only the radio. She switched on again. The phone rang again. Nothing. At last she decided that the ringing was conjured up by her own longing or was some electrical malevolence. The phantom telephone drilled out a shameful memory; last night, among her friends, as the party worn on, alcohol sharpened her loneliness until she dialled his number. Even as she did so she told herself that she would hate herself in the morning. She did. A woman's sleepy voice had answered. She hung up. Boring into their bedroom. Disturbing pink sheets; dreams.

She couldn't read, couldn't watch television, couldn't listen to the radio. She had to admit relief when the children went out that afternoon; when you are a mother, you can't scream that you are dying of loneliness and boredom, that your soul is rotting within you. Let his shadow fall across the glass in the door. Let the telephone ring. She stood at the window for a long time staring at sodden leaves and apples, then she grabbed her coat and went to borrow a dog from a neighbour, a patchy-skinned mongrel called Blue.

Ducks pulled melancholy trails across the dingy lake. It was no better here. When she first met John, people's faces, pavements, skies were irradiated, familiar buildings blossomed with pretty cornices and swags of flowers. Now how ugly and pointless everybody seemed, the whole of Creation a dreary mistake. Damp seeped into her boots, her coat hung open in the cold wind, her bare hands were purple and scratched from the sticks that the fawning Blue laid at her feet to be flung. She glared at the parents trundling past with their prams and tricycles, forgetting that she had been happy once doing that. She found a bench out of the wind and huddled in the corner; the wind whipped the flame from her lighter as she tried to light a cigarette. Ignited, it tasted dirty, the smoke blew into her hair. Without realising it she was rocking slowly back and forth on the bench, head hunched between her shoulders. If only she had never gone to that party in the summer.

'Do you know Dr Frazer?' someone had asked.

'Actually, I'm one of your patients.'

'Oh, I'm sorry . . . I should have recognised you. . . .'

'It's all right, we've never met. I'm never ill.'

'That's a pity.'

She had not met his wife, who was at the far end of the room in a group round the fire, but now, Oh God, wasn't that them coming round the corner. There was no escape.

'Hello.'

The family surrounded her bench. Blue jumped up at John; she saw him wince as the claws raked his thigh. He threw a stick; Blue bolted after it.

'I'm sorry. Your trousers. They're all muddy.'

'Don't worry about those old things! I'm always trying to get him to throw them out, but somehow he always retrieves them!'

Mary gave her a wifely smile; it might as well have been a dead leaf falling or the crisp bag bowling down the path. Mary shivered.

Blue was back with the stick, grinning through frilled red gums.

'I didn't know you had a dog.'

'It's not mine. He belongs to a friend.'

The three children in knitted hats, and Mary, grew impatient. Catherine stood up.

'Goodbye then. Come on Blue.'

John bent over the dog, stroking it inordinately. 'Goodbye, Beautiful.' Fondling its ears.

As Catherine walked away she heard a child's voice say, 'Dad, can we have a dog?'

'Don't you think your mother has enough to do?' his voice snapped, as she had never heard it. Good. I hope your bloody afternoon's ruined. Intruding on her in her ratty fake fur coat, jeans frayed with mud, smoking a cigarette on a park bench, with a borrowed dog; flaunting his family, his wife in her neat tweed coat and matching blue woolly hat. Well, that's that then. It's over. Good. Him in that anorak of horrifying orange. They were welcome to each other. To complete the afternoon's entertainment Mavis Blizzard was bearing down the path pushing part of an old man, wrapped in a tartan rug, in a wheelchair.

When John arrived at the surgery on Monday morning Julie Blizzard was there with her mother.

'Morning, Doctor,' said Mavis.

'Morning, Doctor,' parroted the clone.

He searched his frosty brain for a pleasantry.

'I suppose you'll be leaving school soon, Julie? Any idea of what you want to do?'

'I'm going to work with underprivileged children.'

'They will be,' he muttered as he went through. Then he turned back. 'By the way, Miss Weatherby died on Saturday night.' Or escaped, he might have added.

'Oh dear, the poor soul,' said Mavis absentmindedly. Miss Weatherby merited a small sigh then Mavis added, 'It's the weather, I expect. You know what they say, a green December fills the churchyard. I've got to go over to the hospital myself this afternoon to visit an old boy, that is if he's lasted the night, I'd better check with Sister first. He's blind and his wife's. . . .'

'Doctor,' called Julie after him as he turned away rudely, 'You'll get a surprise when you go into your consulting room!'

Grey, rainy light filtered through white paper cut-out Santas and snowflakes pasted on the window. He punched the black couch where soon a procession of flesh in various stages of decay would stretch out for his inspection, and none of it that which he wanted to see.

Catherine ducked down behind the counter as Mavis Blizzard entered the shop with much jangling of the bell and shook sleety pearls from her plastic hood. When she emerged it was to confront Mary, who gave her a vague smile, as if she thought she ought to know her, and went distractedly from one row of books to another. A pair of wet gloves was placed over Mary's eyes. She gave a little scream. Mavis uncurled her black playful fingers.

'Oh, Mavis! You made me jump!'

As she served people and found and wrapped books Catherine managed to catch snatches of conversation.

'. . . peaky. Down in the dumps.'

'. . . Nothing really. . . .'

'I always start my Christmas shopping in the January sales. Just a few last minute things.'

'. . . he's just tired, I suppose . . . so bad tempered . . . I can't seem to do anything right. . . .'

'You poor little fool,' thought Catherine, 'confiding in that old harridan.'

She stared icily at Mavis as she paid for her book, a reduced volume of freezer recipes, putting the change down on the counter rather than into her hand, but could not kill the thought; I first liked him because he was so kind and now he is less kind because of me.

It was way past the end of Pat's lunch hour. Catherine went into the kitchen and found her, sandwich drooping in her hand, enthralled by the life of a modern saint. She lifted her eyes dreamily from the page.

'Do you know,' she said dreamily, 'she drank the water in which the lepers had washed their feet!'

'I think I'm going to throw up,' said Catherine.

She saw that the sink was clogged with cowslip flowers. Then, at a brawling sound from the street, they both ran back into the shop. A gang of teenagers was rampaging down the pavement, school blazers inside out, garlands of tinsel round their necks and in their hair, which some of them had daubed pink or green. Catherine's eyes blurred at their youth, their faces pink with cold, the flying tinsel. One detached himself and banged on the window.

'Hello, Mum!'

She managed a weak salute.

'Disgusting! No better than animals!' said a customer's voice.

'At least they're alive!' Catherine retorted, because for the moment they were young animals, and not fossicking among freezer recipes and jokey books about golf and fishing.

'I thought she was such a nice girl,' the customer complained to another as they went out.

'It's the other one who's a nice girl,' her friend explained.

'If Blizzard answers, I'll hang up,' Catherine decided as she dialled surgery appointments. One of the underlings took the call. Hers was the last appointment of the evening. She couldn't believe the little scene that was being enacted in the waiting room. Mavis evidently had caught a woman in the act of tearing a recipe from one of the magazines.

'But it is dated 1978 . . .,' the culprit was quavering in her own defence.

'That's not the point. It's the principle of the thing!'

Mavis thrust a pen and a sheet torn from a notepad at her.

'Here, you can copy it out, if you like. If everybody did that. . . .'

It was impossible to see from the woman's bent head if she was writing ground almonds or ground glass, but when her turn to go in came her face was stained a deep red.

Mavis had only Catherine with whom to exchange a

triumphant glance; their eyes met for an instant before she retreated to her sanctum, which, Catherine was amazed to see, was decked with Christmas cards.

'Next Patient for Dr Frazer.'

Catherine went in.

'I knew it! I knew it! I knew something was going on! What do you think I am? Stupid?'

John and Catherine were frozen together as in a freak snowstorm.

'It's disgusting! It's smutty! It's. . . .'

'I realise that's how it must seem to you, but really, I assure you. . . .'

Catherine felt his fingers slide from her breast.

'That's how it appears to me and that's how it is. What do you take me for? I'm not stupid you know.' She turned on Catherine.

'You come here night after night and yet there's never anything written on your card, never any prescription. How do you explain that? Just because you couldn't hold your own husband you try to pinch someone else's! Well, you're not so clever as you think you are, or you, Dr Frazer! Perhaps you'd care to read this?'

She flung an evening paper on the desk. The verdict in the Randal and Peacock case. The condemned pair would not look.

'Guilty, of course. It's his wife I feel sorry for. And the children. What they must be going through! I'd hate Mary to suffer what that poor woman's – '

'You wouldn't!'

'I – ' She had to duck as a paperweight flew past her head and crashed into the door, then Catherine was struggling into her coat.

'Don't go,' he said, but she was gone, blundering through the empty surgery in tears.

A trombone belched outside the window.

'Oh my Gawd, the mince pies!'

Mavis ran from the room as the broken notes of 'Silent Night' brayed. Les Blizzard and his Church Lads' Band had mustered outside to give the doctors a carol.

Someone had rescued Mavis's mince pies, her annual surprise to the doctors, from the little oven she had installed in the office; they were only slightly blackened. The festivities took place in Dr Macbeth's, the senior partner's, room. John looked round: the three receptionists in their blue overalls, Johnson sucking burnt sugar from a painful tooth and trying to smile, Baines eying the bottle, Macbeth, eyes moist with sweet sherry, mincemeat in his white moustache, giving a convincing performance as a lovable old family practitioner, which of course he was. The window, like his own, was decorated with white paper cut-outs. Macbeth raised his glass to Mavis.

'I have heard the Mavis singing.

His love song to the morn.

I have – '

'*Her* love song, surely,' corrected Mavis, reducing his song to a gulp of sherry.

John drained his glass.

'Well, Happy Christmas, everybody. I must be off.'

'But doctor, you haven't pulled your cracker! You can't break up the party yet!'

Mavis was waving the coloured goad in his face. He grasped the end and pulled. 'What is it?' scrabbling among their feet, 'Oh, it's a lucky charm. There, put on your hat!'

She crammed a purple crown on his head; it slipped over his eyes. As he pushed it up, to his horror, he saw a sprig of mistletoe revolving on a thread from the light.

'Ho ho ho,' rumbled Macbeth.

Under cover of the crackers' explosions John muttered, 'Do you think you could remove those bits of paper from my window? They block the light.'

She gave no sign of having heard.

'Oh, I almost forgot! Pressies! You first, Dr Frazer, as you've got to rush off.'

She crammed his weak arms with parcels.

'Just a little something for the children. You'll love little Katy's present! It's a doll that gets nappy rash when it wets itself! Isn't that a hoot? Whatever will they think of next?'

The minions duly hooted.

Catherine watched her ex-husband's feet tangle and tear wrapping paper. He sat down heavily beside her on the floor, pushing parcels out of his way and pulled her to him. His shirt, an obvious Christmas present, perhaps from someone who wished he was with her now, burst open at the neck.

'I still fancy you, you know.'

The whisky smell was like a metal gate across his

mouth. She wanted to howl and weep and, failing John's, any old shirt would do, even this one, smelling so new, with a frill down the front.

'Your shirt. I'm sorry.'

'It doesn't matter. I didn't like it anyway,' pressing a button into her eye.

The bookshop. Mr Hermitage. Pat. Christmas. I'll get through this one, she thought, then the next one and the next. But this will be the worst. The years ahead. Each day that she would not go to the surgery, would not pick up the phone. She saw a series of bleak victories, a lone soldier capturing pointless hills when there was no one to see.

'Do you want to watch the children opening their stockings?'

John realised that she had never had to ask this before; the Christmas tree wavered into a green glass triangle shot with lights; Mary's face, above her pink dressing gown, was pale and wary; she had sensed his absence beside her in bed and come to find him, and now excited sounds were coming from the children's rooms.

'I love you,' he said.

For a moment, before he followed her upstairs, the doctor placed his hand over the pain in his heart. He knew it was incurable.

Drying Out

The gardens were yellow with forsythia and daffodils. All over Surrey choirs were sharpening their throats on Stainer's Crucifixion.

A jug of daffodils stood on the windowsill of the Bull and a cold-scented trumpet grazed Colin's ear as he sat heavily on the chintz bench. Later in the evening he would stick the daffodil behind his ear, but now his first pint was tumbling like a waterfall among his teeth as he laughed at someone's joke.

Slowly the windows darkened as if night was being poured into the bottle-glass by a skilful hand.

At ten o'clock the fire had faded to red lichen on a burnt log. Colin didn't want the evening to end. He lunged at the bar, causing Gerry, the landlord, with a tray of dirty glasses in his hand, to swerve to avoid a woman padding back from the Ladies.

'Shall we dance?'

Diverting a triple collision, Colin grabbed Gerry by the waist and the glasses spun on the tray.

*

Colin arrived at his front door. The porch light had been switched off and the porch was a black mouth sucking him in. A forsythia clawed his face and clashing milk bottles betrayed him to the street. He stood until broken glass settled into jagged silence. The lock took a nip from his finger as he jabbed his key at it.

The hall light beamed a weak searchlight into the interior. A face flashed at him; he stepped back and stared into the gilt-crusted mirror at eyes marbled by cigarette smoke, tiny bubbles of sweat or beer beading the stubble breaking through his chin, a smudge of blood on his cheek.

'I'm home, dear,' he said aloud. 'Daddy's home, every-body!' And snickered.

The oven door clanged open on a brutal, empty smell of oven-cleaner. The fridge brayed as he rifled its cold shelves and seized a fluted pyrex dish containing some sort of flan. He couldn't wait for a knife, but dug in his fingers and gobbled. A lump of pastry lodged in his throat, a grotesque Adam's apple, forcing tears from his eyes as he fought to swallow. A belch tore from his mouth; he could almost see it, a brown beery tornado.

'Pardon me,' he said, licking his fingers.

He pulled the evening paper from his pocket, lit a cigarette and started to read while transferring gobbets from the dish to his mouth almost without noticing. Nothing of interest, some boring drought or famine. He turned the page. The dish slid across the table, he caught at it, but it cracked itself on the edge and he was holding a slice of glass pie in his hand and a mess of glass and food spattered his shoes and the floor.

He knelt and gathered the fragments into a sheet of the newspaper; a black face stared up at him and accused above the words, 'Without your help he will die. . . .' He crumpled it into a clumsy ball and scrubbed at his shoes. He added his burnt-out cigarette and threw the lot into the bin.

The pain in his arm indicated that he had been lying on it for some time. He stretched his pulsating fingers across the sheet and struck emptiness. He felt, in blackness, the space left by Helen's pillow. He groped lower down. Blank sheet. No iron backbone resisting him through thin cotton. It was borne into his sore skull that she had fled with her pillow, but it hurt too much to wonder what drunken crime had propelled her through the dark. The bed stank of beer. He must have water. His pyjama jacket was soaked – a finger found a river running down his breastbone. He pushed back the duvet and rubbed one burning foot against the other. His feet were blurred with socks. O God. Trousers. Not again. Pyjama jacket was sodden shirt. He sat up. His brain lurched; a dry sponge banging against bone, and broken glass, and himself clasped in Gerry's arms dancing with a daffodil behind his ear whirled round in a shameful kaleidoscope.

The blessed water hit the basin and scooped in his hand, hit the roof of his mouth. Handful after handful before it soaked into his palate and began to ease the rusty pipe of his throat. Parched and bloated he hung over the basin trembling at the memory of the venomous liquids he had poured into his body.

At last he raised his dripping face to the mirror of the bathroom cabinet and there, hung in the glass, was a brown face and very slowly a strip of dried leather unrolled between the cracked lips and licked a drop of water on the mirror.

Colin yanked open the door of the cabinet. There stood a reassuring battery of pink and green deodorants, his electric shaver, a pair of silver tweezers. He stared at them, then suddenly slammed the door, as if the deodorants might become bullets, the razor shave more than stubble, the tweezers stab like a stiletto. Turning at the door, he dared look back. The glass was empty.

It was empty because the face had got into the bedroom before him. It loomed closer and closer until he could see the fissures in the lips, count the freckles on the brown skin. Merciful pillow, obliterate. When he opened his eyes the room was light and millions of black specks like freckles swarmed in the air, on the walls, teemed on every surface. He slept.

Surely that was the clash of the kettle lid, the flood of water on aluminium. He lay and waited for the tea to arrive. A fly droned at the window, thudded on the glass, fell back and droned. Red sand thickened in his throat, flies buzzed on eyelids.

'O God, what am I doing to myself? Never again, I swear it. I really mean it this time. O God, where's that bloody tea, I'm dying, help me, someone. . . .'

The sound of the cistern splashed across the ceiling, ran

down the walls, water boomed into the bath, taps' silver hissing, switched on, switched off; the whole house was afloat. And no tea came.

'It's as though I don't exist.'

He stood in the kitchen doorway, his hand on the swaying wall, raking his eyes across the table, the unwashed bowls, the milk bottle's silver cap askew, the cereal packet on its side showing crumpled white underwear, a fly balancing on the sugar bowl's rim.

'Is there any tea in the pot? Where are the kids?'

No answer came from Helen, kneeling in front of the washing machine. His feet felt wet. He was standing in a puddle. Helen stood up and faced him, wet patches on the knees of her jeans. Then she hurled a tangle of wet washing at him; it hit him hard in the stomach and slithered to the floor. She ran into the garden. He stepped over the washing, a tight twist of colour, and paddled across the room making little sucking noises on the floor. He put his hand on the tea pot. It was cold.

Black specks hit him again as he bent to pull a carton of orange juice from the fridge. It was too sweet, but he told himself his body needed the vitamin C as the viscous juice ran down his chin, round his neck, his chest, his wrists. He splashed himself feebly at the sink. The hot water was too hot, the cold didn't wash off the stickiness. He drank a handful with two Disprin. The sun ricocheted off sharp shards of foil on the draining board, blinding him. He groped into the garden. Disorderly green leaves and grass attacked him.

Helen sat hunched on the swing with her back to him,

a white band of skin between her shrunken jumper and her jeans, her hair hanging in a humble hank over each shoulder, her hands trailing. His daughter Holly, wearing only a pair of pants, squatted in a patch of mud digging at it with a plastic spoon. Water dribbled from a green hose at her feet.

'Can we go to the fair this afternoon, Daddy?'

He scooped her up and held her tightly against his chest, feeling the fragile ribs in one hand, softness sitting on his arm, hard little knees scraping his own ribs.

'Sure, darling, I'll take you this afternoon while Mummy does the shopping.'

'Or I could take you while Daddy does the shopping. After he's fixed the washing machine of course. . . .' Helen's words came sourly through her hair.

'Do you have to wear that horrible old jumper? he replied.

'Daddy, you're hurting me! Ow!' as she slid down, a button grazing her skin.

She stood staring up at him, opened her mouth to cry; thought better of it. A vicious pink line like blood-poisoning ran down her chest. She rubbed at it with a muddy hand and crouched down to her digging, backbone sticking out in reproachful knobs.

'Takes after her mother,' thought Colin.

Some self-righteous fool started up a lawn-mower. Then hedge-cutters added their whine. Helen looked slowly from Colin to the waving unkempt glossy grass to the bristling hedge and back at him. He felt his stomach swell to a sickening white puff-ball under her eyes.

An upstairs window opened.

'Dad?'

A wasp bombed his sticky chest. He struck it away.

'O, leave me alone. All of you!' He leapt at the dripping hose, whirling it above his head. The green snake spurted silver venom over the garden. 'Has nobody in this house any idea of the value of water? Don't you know people are dying of thirst?'

Half an hour later, shaven and shaking slightly in a clean shirt, he slammed the car, banged in a cassette and roared away from his intolerable home.

The sun tarnished the flames of the fire in the Bull and polished the dazzling display of brass. For the first time that spring the morning was too hot for a fire. Pale arms like etiolated shoots sprouted from t-shirt sleeves; there was even a pair of shorts on wintry thighs.

'Hair of the dog, old son?'

Two mates were at the bar. Colin clapped an arm round each of their shoulders. Meg, the landlady, unhooked his tankard and a packet of pork scratchings. Her morning lipstick was not yet lubricated to a desirable gloss and it was obvious that she used the same metal polish for her hair and the horsebrasses.

'That hit the spot.'

Colin put down his tankard. Someone kicked the juke-box into song. A daffodil's cold, golden muzzle nuzzled his sleeve, a Jack Russell nipped his calf; he was happy.

At two o'clock the tankard's mouth and Colin's and a little glass's lips were bleared. His greasy face winked at him from the tankard's silver belly. Meg was standing next to him, shimmering like a crocus in a draped dress of silky mauve whose lustre glistened on her eyelids and nails. She placed a purple cigarette in the side of her mouth and as he leaned to light it Colin slid a hand across her hard hip. An ashtray spun like a wheel from his elbow spilling broken spokes of matches and cigarette stubs.

It took him some minutes to realise that he was lying in the park. The last thing he remembered was going out to the Gents.

A square of cerulean blue glittered in the grass. Small bright white columns flanked the white steps leading down to the water. Colin tried the mouth of a dried-up drinking fountain. Then the temptation of the paddling pool overcame him and he stumbled down its steps. A mother roused herself from slapping a toddler to shout at him. His feet crackled over old yogurt cartons in the sandpit as he fled with a mouthful of dead insects and chlorine. On the horizon of his headache white spirits flitted against the green and one flew to catch a ball. Far off a carousel tinkled faintly of his fall.

'The children and I can't stand you any longer. We have gone to my parents'. Food in the freezer. Hope it chokes you.'

The last line was crossed out, but not obliterated.

He crumpled the note and threw it in the bin. Then he cracked open a can of beer and fell asleep in front of the television, and later the night air was fragrant with hot doughnuts as he drove to the Bull.

When Colin got home from work on Monday evening he couldn't face defrosting anything from the freezer. He thought he would get a pie in the pub or perhaps some chicken in a basket or scampi. He couldn't remember anything of the day, before travelling home in the train. He might have been shouting or snoring in the office. His heart was fluttering so only alcohol could calm it. Angst had got into the empty house and swirled like mist through the silent rooms. He would have just one drink to make himself feel better and then telephone Helen.

The clock must have stopped the night before. It said ten-to-eleven and he had only been in the Bull a few minutes. 'You want to have that clock seen to, Gerald.'

Gerry did not deign to answer.

'Here, Gerry, you know those hunger-strikers? I was reading about it on the train. It's not like you think, is it?'

'What's not like you think? You finished with this?'

'When someone dies of hunger, I mean. Or thirst. It's much worse than you think. I mean, I thought you just sort of lapsed into unconsciousness. . . .'

'That's what you're about to do.'

'How do you mean?'

'Lapse into unconsciousness. Come on, sunshine, it's past your bedtime. On your bike.'

Colin could not quite believe that Gerry, if not quite, was as good as throwing him out. He saw his fist tighten

61

round a tea towel. Some mate. Only yesterday they had danced together.

'Sod you too, then. And you can stuff the tankard.'

'Anyway, I haven't got a bike,' he said to the street. He forgot about the car and walked home, anticipating ringing Helen and telling her of Gerry's unpleasantness. But when he got home he forgot.

It seemed that nothing terrible had happened at work. He got through the day creditably. In the train he found himself searching the paper for reports of the drought. Nothing. Probably reports had been much exaggerated. After all, if they had had no rain for four years it was hardly front page news and they must be used to it by now. He walked to the Bull and got his car from the car park. As he passed the window he glimpsed Gerry's blazer and doubtless fake tie. He drove to the Black Lion where he had two whiskies and then dialled Helen's parents' number. There was no reply. Try again later. Two men at the bar were talking about fishing. Colin tuned in.

'Pardon me for butting in, but do you want any maggots?'

'Eh?'

They turned to look at him.

'Do you need any maggots? Only I could let you have some. This evening when I was emptying my rubbish, the pedal bin was crawling with them.'

They moved away.

Colin had another drink and left, calling at the off-licence on his way home.

He fried himself some sausages and eggs and tomato and sat down in front of the television with a glass of whisky at his foot. A row of naked children were squatting in the dust cramming what appeared to be Farex into their mouths with their hands, smearing it over their lips, turning up and licking their empty bowls. His own kids could never stand the stuff. . . . A white bullock keeled over into the red dust, nothing but eyes and flies and strips of flesh glued to bones that at any moment might cut through. He contrasted it with the plump sausage on his fork.

A little later he rang Helen. The line was engaged. Great. That meant she was trying to get through to him. He would wait. And waited until he woke in his chair at one o'clock. He drained his glass and blundered to bed. His brain felt like an old wasps' nest, all ideas dead or flown, the cells dried to brittle paper.

A wasps' nest was bowled by a hot wind along the bed of a dried-up river where cracked mud stood up in slabs of evil, yellow crazy paving, and a man crouched poking at the crust with a twig no thicker than his arm.

Colin woke before he could raise his face, because he could not have borne to look into those yellow eyeballs streaked with red. He wished he had thought to place a glass of water at his bedside.

Not a glass, not a bucketful, not a crystal river could irrigate him now. Send Lazarus that he may dip his finger. . . .

There was a letter in a brown envelope addressed to Helen. He opened it.

63

'Today millions of women will trudge miles in blistering heat to fetch water. It will be teeming with invisible germs and parasites. But their families will drink it anyway – they have no choice. Every day 30,000 people die because of the lack of clean drinking water. The death toll in one year is ten million.'

He rang in sick. Eleven o'clock found him at the Oxfam shop with a pound note at the ready. It was closed.

It seemed that he was back in the Bull. Neither he nor Gerry referred to the incident of a few nights ago. Meg leaned over the bar.

'I don't mean to pry. I mean, tell me to mind my own beeswax if you like, but is anything the matter? At home, I mean? You don't look well.'

'No, no.'

At the word beeswax a dried out wasps' nest bowled into his mind.

'Just a glass of Adam's ale for me this morning, Meg.'

'A pint of Adnam's? Coming up.' She reached for his tankard.

'No, no, I meant water.'

'Water? You are in a bad way.'

'Thanks, Meg. How much do I owe you?'

'Have it on the house. It's only water.'

'It's bloody typical,' Colin heard his own voice much later, ' – same again, thank you Gerry, and one for your good self – absolutely typical, you try to help these people and the bloody shop's shut!'

'Give it a rest, Colin, you're beginning to be a bore. Anyway, charity begins at home, I always say.'

'Gerry's right, dear,' said Meg. 'It's not really being kind in the long run. If they just depend on us all the time. They've got to help theirselves.'

'The money never gets there anyway. It's all spent on advertising.'

'Anyway, what about the urban deprivation in our own inner cities?' someone else joined in. 'Never mind the Third World. . . .'

'Or the handicapped. In this, the Year of the Disabled – I was at a Lions' Do only the other night and. . . .'

'Yeah, but, the price of this packet of fags,' Colin was almost weeping, 'the price of these fags could restore someone's sight to blindness.'

At the guffaw which met this tears did come to his eyes and he turned away.

'They ought to stand on their own feet.'

'If they've got any,' Colin muttered.

'Here, stick something in this if it will salve your conscience.'

A lifeboat ploughed through wooden waves towards him. Colin dropped in two pence.

'Anyway, what do you think they'd do for us, if we was starving? F-all.'

Holly was walking up the road in front of him. A tiny figure in shorts alone in the High Street. She stopped in front of the petshop as his thudding feet caught up with her.

'Holly!'

She turned. A face as flat and round as a red frisbee. Familiar shorts and t-shirt had deceived. Colin fell to his knees.

'Are those Mothercare shorts?' he asked tenderly.

'Get lost, you pervert.'

The child was yanked from danger.

A blue and yellow feather from a tragic macaw drifted out of the petshop.

Better late than never. Eleven o'clock of the next morning found Colin on the concourse of Victoria Station. As he fought foreigners and luggage trolleys and sleeping bags to reach the entrance of the tube, a hand gripped his arm. A brown face was staring into his. Sounds and colours fused to a dazzle, he was falling . . . he swayed, supported on floppy legs by his accuser.

'You feeling all right, mate? I was only going to ask if you had a spare cigarette.'

A wet butt fell from Colin's lips as he shook his head dumbly, wrenched free and barged into a deranged derelict with a pair of tights on his head.

Then he was caught between the backpacks of two passing Canadians, the helpless meat in a canvas and aluminium sandwich, and deposited in the doorway of the Belgravia bar.

'O well, better even later than even more never. Or words to that effect.'

In the Gents he reminded himself: My name is Colin.

My wife is called Helen. I have two children called Ben and Holly. I am on my way to work.

He wondered if any of it was true.

Late that evening he woke on Ben's bed to the glassy reproach of a teddy bear's eyes in the moonlight. The stairs reared up sickeningly at him as he stumbled towards the medicine in his briefcase at their foot.

'Anything on telly?'

'Nothing worth watching as usual,' he replied, switching it on, and dozed through the news.

'There seems to be no respite in the suffering of the people of drought-stricken Lomasia. The long-awaited rains have brought severe flooding and hundreds of refugees are reported drowned –'

'Thank God. O, thank God.'

He jumped from his chair, kicking over his glass, then sank back, his head in his hands, rocking with dry sobs.

The whisky soaked into the carpet and the damned matchstick men and their diseased cattle were swept away in a yellow torrent. One last sight of his tormentor's bloated face as it whirled past a vulture on the tip of a cracked tree and was gone.

A letter from Helen came in the morning. They were returning that afternoon because the children had to go back to school.

Leaving behind a cleaned-up house and dead bottles discreetly shrouded in plastic bags in the dustbin, Colin, sober and healed by hours and hours of wonderful blank sleep, set off on foot, he felt the need to walk, to lay in supplies. He was slightly weak and convalescent and without his familiar false unfocused spectacles of alcohol everything and everybody shimmered in the clear air. He almost swooned in a waft of grinding coffee and new bread. Fresh orange juice sloshed virtuously inside him. He called at the electrical repair shop to arrange for the washing machine, the remembrance of whose broken state had set his stomach lurching like its broken drum, to be fixed. Behind him in the launderette sheets, towels, shirts and an injudiciously added pair of jeans idled in an indigo haze. He went to the bank.

In the newsagent's he blinked as the sun struck the facets of a pile of red and blue and gold eggs. Price reduced.

'Have we had Easter?'

The assistant looked at him strangely.

'I'll take those two.'

He pointed at the biggest golden eggs in the most splendid boxes.

Colin put down on the pavement his two carrier bags and let the breeze flap his shirt under his arms. He was sweating and thirsty. He looked at his watch. Two hours before they were home. Surely he deserved a little reward after all his hard work. Surely it wasn't right for a heart to race like that. Something to calm it, a soothing shandy. Something therapeutic – he owed it to Helen to be calm. . . .

He placed the eggs carefully on the bar.

'For my kids,' he explained to Meg. 'They've been on

holiday.' In a bungalow in Coulsdon, he might have added but the word holiday evoked white sails and sands and seas sparkling like the carbonated rainbows spiralling in Meg's glass.

Space Invaders invaded; feathered darts flew.

'One for the road. Mustn't keep them waiting.' He knocked it back and hurried into the sunshine.

As he lunged round the corner one of the carrier bags caught the edge of the tray of a man selling paper flowers for a charity, sending an explosion of pink petals against the blue sky.

'Don't worry! Don't worry, I'll take the lot.'

Colin grabbed a shower of flowers from the air, the pavement, and jamming a ten pound note in the slot of the tin, rammed a bunch of pins into his lapels.

'Charity begins at home, I always say.'

He laughed a gust of whisky into the vendor's open mouth.

As he picked up his bags he saw that one of the Easter eggs was dented, its foil torn and the bloom of melting chocolate smearing its gold. Nothing that a little sellotape couldn't cure.

Decked with flowers, hands bleeding from a dozen tiny pinpricks, he fairly danced with his shopping up the hill to greet his family.

Pink Cigarettes

As the cab dawdled down Pimlico Road Simon slithered and fretted on the polished seat. The shops, which had so recently enchanted him with glimpses of turquoise and mother-of-pearl and chandeliers spouting jets of crystal lustres against dark glass, now threatened him with a recurrence of his old complaint, boredom. He looked neither to the left nor the right lest he see again a certain limbless torso, a gilded dodo or a headless stone lion holding out a truncated paw. Surely it would be kinder to put it out of its misery? He saw himself administering the *coup de grâce* with a mallet and sighed, and closed his eyes but was too late to escape the sight of two Chelsea Pensioners lurking like wind-bitten unseasonal tulips among the grey graves of the Royal Hospital. He pulled off his red tie and stuffed it into his pocket. His misery was complete as they crossed Kings Road and he turned from the fortunates on the pavement in their pretty clothes to his own reflection in a small mirror; nobody, he feared, could call him yesterday's gardenia, more like yesterday's beefburger in a school blazer. He had been forced to leave the house in his uniform, and he had a cold. He had poisoned his ear with a cheap ear-ring and it throbbed with the taxi's motor.

He thought that this was the most unpleasant cab in which he had ever ridden – a regular little home-from-home with a strip of freshly hoovered carpet on the floor, a photograph, dangling from the driver's mirror, of two cute kids daring him to violate the *Thank you for not smoking* sign, and a nosegay of plastic flowers in a little chrome vase exuding wafts of Harpic. He remembered with envy a taxi ride he had once taken with his mother; she had had no time to look out of the window or be bored. She had replenished lipstick and mascara and combed her hair and then she had taken from her bag a bottle of pungent pink liquid and a tissue and rubbed the varnish from her nails, decided against repainting them, and lit a cigarette and when she had stubbed it out on the discarded tissue, the ashtray had gone up in flames. It had been lovely.

He was thrown forward when the cab braked suddenly as the car in front pulled into a parking space.

'Woman driver!' said the cab driver.

'Or a transvestite,' said Simon.

The driver did not reply, but added ten pence to the clock after he had stopped. Simon ran down the steps, hoping to avoid being spotted by the housekeeper, who had taken an unaccountable dislike to the slender blond, amanuensis of the tenant of the basement flat.

'Don't kiss me, I've got a cold,' he greeted the old poet who opened the door. The cocktail cabinet was closed; that was always a bad sign. He wondered if he dared risk opening it while the old man was pottering about in the kitchen, dunking a sachet of peppermint tea in a cup of boiling water.

'Simon?'

He lounged in the doorway wasting a winning smile on his host.

'Would you like a tisane?'

'Wouldn't mind something a bit stronger. . . .'

'There's some Earl Grey in that tin,' said the cruel old buzzard who was dressed today in shades of cream, with a natty pair of sugared almonds on his feet and a dandified swirl of clotted cream loosely knotted at his throat and a circlet of gold-rimmed glass pinned with a milky ribbon to his wide lapel. Simon became conscious again of his own drab garb.

'Sorry about the clothes,' he said sulkily, 'my mother was around when I left so I. . . .'

'I've told you before, dear boy, it doesn't matter in the least what you wear.'

Simon was not mollified. He watched him lower his accipitrine head appreciatively into the efflorescence from his cup, complacently ignoring as usual the risks Simon took on his behalf, and risks for what? He stared out of the window at a few thin early snowflakes melting on the black railings.

'Snow in the suburbs,' he said.

'I should hardly call this the suburbs.'

'It was a literary allusion.'

'Not a very apt one, as anyway it has stopped snowing. Now, are you going to have some tea, or shall we get straight down to work? We've got a lot to get through today.'

'*We,*' echoed Simon bitterly and sneezed.

'I expect that lake of yours is frozen this morning?' added the poet.

'Not quite.' Simon proffered a stained shoe.

'I've got an old pair of skates somewhere. I must disinter them for you.'

Simon, who thought that they were already on thin ice, drummed his nails on the windowpane. The scent that had intrigued him early in their acquaintance he knew now to be mothballs and it was coming strongly off the white suit.

'You're very edgy this morning. For goodness sake stop fidgeting and pour yourself some absinthe, as you insist on calling it.'

With three boyish bounds Simon was at the cocktail cabinet smiling at himself in its mirrored back as he poured Pernod into a green glass. It was amazing how good he looked, when he had felt so ugly before. Was he really beautiful or was there a distortion in the glass, or did the poet's thinking him beautiful make him so? He could have stood for an indefinite length of time reflecting, sipping his drink, a cocktail Sobranie completing the picture but the old man came into the room casting his image over the boy's. Simon turned gracefully from the waist.

'Got any pistachios, Vivian?'

'No.'

'You always used to buy me pistachios,' he whined.

'It would take my entire annual income, which, as you

know, is not inexhaustible, to keep you in pistachio nuts, my dear. Now, to work.'

Simon gazed in despair at the round table under the window spilling the memorabilia of more than eighty years; diaries, khaki and sepia photographs, yellow reviews that broke at a touch, letters from hands all dead, all dead, with here and there a flattened spider or a fly's wing between the brittle pages, or the ghost of a flower staining the spectral ink, into boxes and files and pools of paper on the floor. Simon shuddered. His task was to help to put them into chronological order so that the poet might complete his memoirs, while the little gold clock that struck each quarter made it ever more unlikely that he would. He plunged his hand into a box and pulled out a photograph of a baby in a white frock riding on a crumpled knee, which, if it could be identified, would no doubt belong to someone very famous. He tried to smooth it with his hand.

'Do be careful, Simon! These things are very precious!'

'It's not my fault!' Simon burst out. 'I don't really know what I'm supposed to be looking for, and when I do manage to put anything in order, you snatch it away from me and mess it all up again!'

'What? Listen, Simon, I want to read something to you. Go and sit down. Have a cigarette. Are you old enough to smoke, by the way? There are some by your chair. Light one for me.'

Simon gloomed over the cigarettes, like pretty gold-tipped pastels in their black box, not knowing which to choose. He had expected tea at the Ritz and hock and seltzer at the Cadogan Hotel, and here he was day after day grubbing through musty old papers for a book that would never be finished, that no one would publish if it was finished, and that no one would read if it was published. . . .

'Of course it never occurs to some people that some other people are going to fail all their 'O' Levels,' he muttered.

'No, we didn't have 'O' Levels when I was at school,' agreed Vivian. 'Listen Simon, this will interest you. . . .' The words spilled like mothballs from his mouth and rolled around the room, '"and so I set foot for the first time on Andalusian soil, a song in my heart, a change of clothing in my knapsack, a few pesetas in my pocket, travelling light, for the youthful hopes and ideals that made up the rest of my baggage weighed but little" – you might at least pretend to be awake. . . .'

'I am. Please go on, that last bit was really poignant.'

'Oh, do you think so, Simon, I'm so glad. I rather hoped it was.'

Simon selected a pink cigarette, and wondering if it was possible to pretend to be awake, fell fast asleep. He woke with a little cry as the cigarette blistered his fingers.

'I thought that would startle you,' chuckled the poet, 'you didn't expect that of me, did you?'

'I don't know. . . .'

What deed it had been, of valour or romance, he would never know, but his reply pleased the old man.

'Come on, I'll take you out for a drink, and then we'll have some lunch.'

*

Simon attracted some attention in his school blazer in the Coleherne Arms.

'This is a really nice pub,' he told Vivian, 'do you know, three people offered to buy me a drink while you were in the Gents?'

The poet stalked out, the black wings of his cloak flapping and smiting people and Simon had to scramble up from the dark corner where he had been seated and follow him.

Much later, as he ran across the concourse at Victoria and lunged at the barrier he collided with a friend of his mother, on her way to her husband's firm's annual dinner dance in a long dress and fur coat, a dab of Home Counties mud on her heels.

There was nobody in. That is to say, his parents were out. Simon made himself a sandwich and took it upstairs. His room was as he had left it; the exploded crisp bags, the used mugs and glasses, the empty can of Evo-Stik, the clothes and comics, records and cassettes on the floor untouched by human foot, for no one entered it but he. He looked out of the window, and the pond in the garden below, glittering dully in the light from the kitchen provoked an image of himself curvetting round its brackish eighteen-inch perimeter on a pair of archaic silver skates. He shivered and pulled the curtain, vowing feebly once again to extricate himself as he flopped down on the bed. When he had met the poet, not expecting the acquaintance to last more than an afternoon, he had constructed grandiose lies about his antecedents and house and garden, and had sunk a lake in its rolling lawns. He became aware of the sound of lapping wavelets; somebody next door was taking a bath, and he felt loneliness and boredom wash over him.

It was boredom that had led to his first timid ring on the poet's bell. One afternoon, in Latin, deserting from the Gallic Wars and tired of the view from the window, the distant waterworks like a grey fairground where sea gulls queued for rides on its melancholy roundabouts, he had taken from his desk a book; an anthology whose faded violet covers opened on names as mysterious as dried flowers pressed by an unknown hand. Lascelles Abercrombie, whom some wit, in memory or anticipation, of school dinner, had altered to Brussels Applecrumble, Vivian Violett – Simon selected him as the purplest, and turned the pages to his poem.

'What's that you're reading, Simon?'

'It's only an old book I found in the lost property cupboard.' Simon lifted tear-drenched eyes to the spectacles of the master who had oozed silently to his side.

'Let me see. My goodness, Vivian Violett! That takes me back. . . .'

'Is he good, sir?'

'I think that this is, er, what's known as a good bad poem. . . .'

He wove mistily away, adjusting his headlights, shaking

his head as if to dislodge the voices of nightingales from his ears.

'Is he dead, sir?' Simon called after him.

'Oh, undoubtedly, undoubtedly. Isn't everyone? You could check in *Who's Who*, I suppose.'

'You are a creep, Si,' whispered the girl sitting next to him, 'I got a detention for reading in class.'

'Of course,' said Simon.

'Poseur,' she hissed.

'Moi?'

At the last count, Simon, for whom the word *decadence* was rivalled in beauty only by *fin-de-siècle*, found that Vivian Violett was alive and living in London.

The next day he climbed the steps of an immense baroque biscuit hung with perilous balconies and blobs of crumbling icing, to present himself in the role of young admirer. His disappointment at being redirected to the basement by a large weevil or housekeeper in an overall was tempered when Vivian Violett opened his door, an eminently poetic Kashmir shawl slung round his velvet shoulders and scrutinised him through a gold-rimmed monocle clamped to the side of his beak and a cloud of smoke and some other exotic perfume. The poet was charmed by his guest.

'I do enjoy the company of young people,' he sighed, 'especially when they're as pretty as you. . . .'

Simon reclined on faded silk, fêted with goodies, not yet knowing that he was not only the only *young* person, but almost the *only* person to have crossed the threshold for many years.

'You must tell me all about yourself,' Vivian said, at once swooping and darting into his own past to peck out tarnished triumphs and ancient insults, shuffling names like dusty playing cards; a mechanical bird whose rusty key had been turned and who could not stop singing. From time to time he cocked his head politely at Simon's poor attempts, over a rising mound of pistachio shells, to attribute a little grandeur to himself before flying again at the bookcase to pull down some fluttering album of photographs or inscribed volume of verse to lay them at Simon's feet. It was then that the idea of Simon helping with the memoirs was born. A faint murmur about having to go to school was brushed aside like a moth.

'Nonsense, dear boy. You will learn so much more with me than those dullards could ever teach you. Besides, I have so little time. . . .'

Simon was struck with sadness; the figure dwindling to a skeleton in its embroidered shawl had been, by its own account, the prettiest boy in London. Already he had noticed in himself a tendency to grow a little older each year.

'You will come and see me again soon, won't you?' the poet pleaded.

'Very soon,' promised Simon over the ruins of a walnut cake.

'Such a pity one can't get Fuller's walnut cake any more,' mourned Vivian for the third time.

'Mmm,' agreed Simon again, without knowing in the least what he was talking about.

'I hope you don't find this too cloying, Simon,' resorting

80

to a tiny ivory toothpick, a splinter of some long-departed elephant.

Simon was dribbling the last drops from his glass onto some dry crumbs on his plate and licking them off his finger; the effect was agreeable, like trifle.

'Do you know that poem of mine "Sops in Wine"? Of course you must, it's in the *Collected Works*,' – a volume which Simon had claimed to possess and which he had glimpsed only on a shelf of one of the tottering bookcases which lined the room – 'I'll say it to you.' And he laid back his lips like an old albino mule and brayed out the verse, sing-song in a spray of crumbs.

Simon reached for the decanter of madeira as if it might drown the sound of the last plausible train pulling out of Victoria, for he had not told his parents of his proposed visit. He need not have worried because when he telephoned home they had gone out.

That had been the first of his visits, and as he lay, weeks later, on his bed wondering how he could make the next one the last, toying with the idea of a severe illness, the telephone rang. He had difficulty at first in recognising the voice of his best friend.

'Do you want to come round to my place?' he was asking.

'Okay, I'll be round in ten minutes.'

But as he was leaving the house the phone rang again.

'Oh Simon, I've just had such an unpleasant encounter with the housekeeper, complaints of playing my radio too loudly, accusations of blocking the drains with bubbles, I

mean to say, have you ever heard of anything so ridiculous
. . . all lies of course, you know she wants to get me out, it's
all a conspiracy with the landlord so that he can re-let at a
grossly inflated price. Bubbles! What would you do with
such people, Simon? I know what I'd do, you must come
and see me tomorrow, Simon, I'm so upset and lonely and
blue. . . .'

'I really can't. I've really got to go to school.'

'Well have dinner with me then at least.'

'I haven't got the fare,' said Simon weakly, 'my building
society account's all. . . .'

'Of course I shall give you some more money tomorrow,
you should have reminded me.'

'I've got to go. The phone's ringing. I mean, there's
someone at the door!'

On his way to school the following morning Simon was
overtaken by his friend Paul.

'What happened to you last night? I thought you were
coming round?'

'I was, only I got depressed. . . .'

'Old Leatherbarrow's been asking about you, you know.
Why haven't you been at school? Are you ill or something?'
You don't look too good.'

Suddenly school was an impossible prospect.

'I don't think I'll come in today after all.'

'Well, what shall I tell him? He keeps on at me! He'll
be phoning your parents soon!' Paul's voice rose among
the traffic.

'That's all right, they're never in. Tell him I'm suffering from suspected hyperaesthesia. I'm waiting the results of tests. Don't worry, I'll sort it out.'

He turned and left Paul standing on the pavement exhaling clouds of worried steam.

'Simon, it was sweet of you to come!'

Simon was shocked to see him still in his dressing gown, albeit one of mauve silk with a dragon writhing up its back, and a pair of unglamorous old men's pajamas. The flat smelled stale, like a hothouse where the orchids have rotted.

'Aren't you going to get dressed?' he asked disapprovingly, being young enough to think that if a person was old or ill it was because he wanted to be so.

'I will, now that you're here,' said Vivian meekly. 'I wasn't feeling very bright this morning.' His hand shook and a purple drop spilled to the carpet as he handed Simon a conical glass of parfait amour.

'Ah, meths,' said Simon, 'my favourite.'

'What are you grinning at?'

'Old Leatherbarrow. The St Lawrence Seaway. . . .' replied Simon enigmatically. The forced daffodils which he had brought on an earlier visit hung in dirty yellow tags of crêpe paper against a small grisaille.

'Why have you been so ratty lately?'

'Have I? I'm so sorry Simon if I should have appeared to be ratty towards you, of all people, the person in the world to whom I should least like to be ratty when I am so grateful to have your friendship and your help. I suppose I have been worried. A thousand small unpleasantnesses with the housekeeper, and most of all about this . . .' he waved a hand at the tower of papers on the table. ' "Time's winged chariot . . ." and Christmas. . . .'

'Christmas?' said Simon, 'Christmas is okay – ' and stopped.

'I shall go and dress now. Can you amuse yourself for a few minutes? Then perhaps we could do a little work on the memoirs. Where did we leave them?'

'You had just enlisted in the 'nth Dragoons,' he said as Vivian disappeared into the bedroom. Simon entered with a drink as he was impaling a cravat with a nacreous pin.

'Ah, my little Ganymede,' said the poet, smiling palely, 'what should I do without you?'

It was raining when they set out that evening for the Indian restaurant round the corner.

'Oh dear, oh dear, where's my umbrella? Simon, haven't you got a hat?'

'Of course not.'

'We don't want you to catch another cold. You'd better wear this.' He placed a large soft fedora on Simon's head. 'Yes, it suits you very well.'

Simon smiled at himself in the glass. He wondered if Vivian minded that the hat looked so much better on him.

A fake blue Christmas tree had been set in the restaurant window and cast a bluish light on the heavy white table cloth and imparted a spurious holiness to the bowls of spoons and the candle holder by staining them the rich deep blue of church glass. Two pink cigarettes were smoking themselves in the ashtray. In an upstairs room across the street, behind a sheet looped across the window, an ayatollah or mullah was leading a congregation of men in prayer; their heads rose and fell. Simon felt suddenly the sharp happiness of knowing that, for a moment, he was perfectly happy. He smiled over his wine at Vivian. The old man gripped the handles of his blue spoon and fork.

'I don't think I can bear,' he said, 'to spend another Christmas alone in that flat.'

'But it's a lovely flat,' answered Simon inadequately and then there was silence while the waiter brought the food.

'I can't face any more unpleasantness. Days and days of not seeing you. . . .'

'Mushroom bhaji?'

'No. No. You help yourself.'

Simon looked with embarrassment at his own heaped plate but was too hungry not to spear a surreptitious forkful and tried not to look as if he was chewing. He crumbled a poppadum while he tried to think of something to say.

'Do you know what I have been thinking?'

The poppadum turned to ashes in Simon's mouth.

'Why don't I spend Christmas with you?'

Simon choked on unimaginable horrors; carols round the telly, stockings suspended from a storage heater, a mournful quartet in paper hats silently pulling crackers, Vivian crushed like a leaf between his parents, in bulky, quilted body-warmers, asking for parfait amour at the bar of the local; their sheer incomprehension. . . .

'What do you think, Simon?'

When he could speak he muttered desperately, 'I'm not sure that you'd get on with my parents.'

'We have one thing in common anyway, so that's a good start.'

'They're really boring. We never do anything much. You'd be bored out of your mind.'

'I'm never bored when we're together. Besides a quiet family Christmas is just what I need, what I've missed all these years. We could do some work on the memoirs. I'm sure your parents would be interested. We could go for long walks, that would be very good for me, and you could introduce me to your friends. What do you say?'

'I –'

'It's a large house, as you've told me, so I shouldn't be in the way.'

Simon had to stop him before he actually begged. Maybe his train would crash tonight, maybe his parents would have run away. . . .

'I think it's a great idea,' he said, raising his glass, 'I'll tell them tomorrow.'

Vivian had to apply his napkin to his eye. He reached for Simon's hand and pressed it, then fell with a sudden appetite on the cold food in the silvery blue dishes.

'I wonder where those skates have got to?' he mused. 'Must be in a box somewhere, on top of a bookcase or under the bed. Ring me tomorrow when you've spoken to your parents, won't you?'

He put Simon in a taxi, and he was driven away with a despairing flourish of the black fedora through the window.

Simon could not ring him the next day, which was Saturday, because of course he had not spoken to his parents. On Sunday he woke late from a nightmare of Pickwickian revelry on the garden pond to the realisation that he had left the hat on the train. He went downstairs to find a message in his mother's hand on the pad by the telephone: 'Violet Somebody rang. Can you call her back?'

'They're delighted,' he told Vivian on the telephone, tenderly fingering the lump on his head where he had banged it on the wall. 'I can't talk now, but I'll come to see you tomorrow.'

He arrived hatless, sick with guilt, a dozen excuses fighting in his brain, clutching a paper cone of freezing violets, at Vivian's house. Before he could descend the steps the housekeeper flung open the front door.

'If you want to see Mr Violett, you're too late. They've taken him away.'

'What?'

'Last night. It seems he was climbing up on some steps to get something off the bookcase. Pulled the whole lot down on top of himself. There was an almighty crash, I dashed downstairs with my pass-key, in my nightie, but there was nothing I could do. It seems the actual cause of death was a blow to the head from an ice skate.'

A stout woman, wearing if not actual, spiritual jodphurs, appeared on the step beside her. 'This is Mr Violett's great-niece. She's taken charge of everything.'

As Simon turned and ran he thought he heard the great-niece boom, 'Of course he was always a third-rater,' and the housekeeper reply, 'Oh, quite.'

He hailed a passing cab, and as he sat, still holding his violets, he saw that the windscreen carried the Christmas lights of Sloane Square in a little coloured wreath all the way to Eaton Square. 'There must be a good bad poem somewhere in that' he said to himself.

'The Headmaster would like to interview you, Simon, about your frequent absences.'

Simon knocked dully on the door, stuffing his handkerchief into his trouser pocket, his heart and thoughts miles away.

'Don't kiss me, I've got a cold,' he said, then saw in the mirror behind the astonished pedagogue the reflection of a red-eyed schoolboy in a blazer, whose crying had brought out spots on his nose, and as he pulled out his handkerchief again, saw a broken pink cigarette fall to the floor, and an irrecoverable past diminishing in the glass, when he had been Ganymede for a little while.

Curry at the Laburnums

Rain set in. The hills were hidden and the village enclosed in dull grey curtains of mist. The river threatened the supports of the bridge. Children gauged the water level, hoping, as sometimes happened, that they would be cut off from school. The playground was roofed over by umbrellas, floral patterned, transparent pagodas, under which waiting mothers complained. Little, inadequate sandbags appeared outside some houses. Fields lay under a glaze of water. Some cows were temporarily marooned and a rotten tree trunk, caught under the bridge, bobbed uncannily like the head of a drowned cow. The river continued to rise, grass and nettles disappeared and alders stood in water which poured over the sides of the bridge and reduced the road to a narrow sluice.

Commuters returning to houses draped with wet washing were bored and alienated by tales of muddy dramas, trees swept downstream, rescued water rats, coaches forcing their way through the water and taking children miles round the back roads to school. They were more interested to hear that water had got into the cellars of the pub. They became a different species from the gumbooted inhabitants of the heart of the flood, irritated by wives shut up all day with small children and felt that the trials of water in the brakes, an abandoned car rota, and a go-slow on the trains were far greater than those of the home front.

The platform was jammed. What many found hardest to bear was the unfailing cheerfulness of Lal, the ticket collector, with whom Ivor, from vague liberal principles, often made a point of speaking, exchanging comment on the weather, and last Christmas he had thrust, almost aggressively, a pound note into his hand. Since the go-slow, he somehow hadn't liked to be seen chatting at the ticket collector's box and had restricted himself to a curt nod.

Lal laughed and joked and even made mock announcements over his microphone. Many were quite indecipherable, and the packed, soaked travellers eagerly turning to gaze at the signal which still showed red, and hearing his high-pitched cackle crackling over their heads, stared angrily up the receding tracks and understood only that they had been duped. In his efforts to entertain them, Lal had brought along his own transistor radio from home and played it loud enough to cheer up those at the farthest ends of the platforms. Many of them seemed not to appreciate Radio One.

'I wonder if you know that it's illegal to play transistor radios in public places?' a lady asked, shaking a rain-drop from her nose.

'Must keep my customers happy,' he replied. She reported him to the Station Manager who told him to turn it off.

'Bolshie so-and-so, playing the radio while his fellow Reds hold us to ransom.' A voice was heard in the aftermath.

'Blacks, more like,' replied another.

Camaraderie flowered among the wet heads and shoulders as stranger muttered to stranger imprecations on Blacks and Reds. Ivor and Roger Henry, his neighbour and old school-friend, were edging along the platform to try to get some sense out of Lal. He seized his microphone and shouted:

'All passengers Wictoria and Vaterloo, you might as well go home,' and cackled. Then, as the two men reached his box, he received a telephone announcement, the signal went green and he called: 'All Stations Wictoria. Stopping train Wictoria!'

Twenty minutes later, the grateful commuters saw the train's round caterpillar face crawling towards them and those who could, fought their way aboard and stood steamily, agonisingly pinioned together, fainters held upright, pregnant women loathed for their bulk, dead limbs slowly filling with pins and needles, trapped ever tighter by a seemingly impossible influx at subsequent stations.

So it went on. Drivers reported late and were sent home. Rule books ruled. Trains ran spasmodically. At least the rain began to peter out and there were occasional flashes of watery sunshine.

Ivor and Roger were on the platform, at the edge of a group of older men, doyens of commuting, whose trousers were of necessity hoisted high over round bellies by braces and fell in soft cuffs onto polished shoes, whose muscles were adapted only to the hoovering of lawns with electric

91

mowers, or hitting golf balls; electors who kept Chubleigh a safe Tory seat. At election times its windows broke out in a blue rash of posters depicting Sir John Upton, who seemed to be conjured up only then, opposed only by an occasional doomed orange placard.

'. . . Harold Wilson,' Ivor caught.

'Heh heh heh,' laughed the old boys; products of small schools set back under the dripping beeches of Surrey. A pekinese-faced lady, with steel-blue fur brushed up from a pink powdered forehead, bared her little teeth and laughed.

'Just let them try to treat cattle like this,' said one, 'and they'd soon have all the do-gooders up in arms.'

Their two weeks of inconvenience led these men, holding briefcases packed with the data of unnecessary companies, to compare themselves with Jews transported across Poland in freezing cattle trucks. One licked his livery lips, spotted like sloughed snake skins, and said:

'Did you hear about the Epsom incident? Some chaps got hold of one of those blighters and locked him in the, er, Ladies.'

'Heh heh heh,' laughed the old boys.

'Ha ha,' laughed Ivor.

'Next train to Vaterloo approaching Platform One in about twenty minutes,' broadcast Lal.

No train materialised. Some people went home. The coffee machine was jammed; a squirt of dirty water rattled into the plastic cup. Ivor and Roger trailed after the group to a little shack in the forecourt which sold such fare as sausage sandwiches, sulphurous rock cakes and tea. They blocked the doorway and jostled the taxi-drivers seated on benches round the walls, shooting spray over them as they closed their umbrellas, and brayed at the woman in broken slippers frying bacon at the stove. The kettle was shrieking; all was steam, noise and succulent wisps of smoke.

'What's yours, Tony?'

'Name your poison.'

'Your shout, I believe, you old rascal.'

'Heh heh heh.'

The woman removed the whistle from the kettle and unfortunately the words, '. . . Bloody unhygienic, ought to be prosecuted' hung in the air.

A huge man in shirtsleeves hoisted himself up from the bench.

'Right,' he said. 'Everybody out. We don't want your sort here. You're all barred!'

'Now look here . . .'

'Out.'

The taxi-drivers rose, a menacing semi-circle confronting former customers.

'Well really, I must say. . . .'

'Out.'

'Now look here, my dear chap, it says "ALL WELCOME" outside. Do you realise you're contravening the Trades Descriptions Act?'

'We demand to be served,' said Ivor from the back.

'Berks.'

The drivers stepped forward. The commuters retreated.

'If that's their attitude. . . .'

Step by step, the commuters were forced backwards

into the forecourt, out of the delicious smell of bacon and hot tea into the cold drizzle.

'Good mind to call the police.'

'Well, I for one shall be contacting the Inspector of Health and I suggest you all do the same.'

A stomach brayed expressing everyone's disappointment.

'My wife was sold a mouldy pie the other day,' volunteered Roger and was ignored.

Ivor felt specially outraged, like a little boy who arrives late for school dinner and finds the hatches closed and his comrades wiping gravy and custard from their lips. Marian had neglected to make muesli and he had left with only a small, bitter cup of coffee. He and Roger went back through the booking hall and found themselves at Lal's box. Ivor was lightheaded and on the point of telling Roger he was giving up and going home. His mouth opened and hung open. Surely not? It couldn't be – a hot pungent drift of curry caught his nose. He stood swooning as it washed over his empty stomach. Roger caught his arm.

' The last bloody straw.'

He looked. The youngest porter, a lowly boy in a too-big jacket, who swept the platforms, was crossing the line bearing foil dishes of take-away curry.

'As you say, the last straw.'

Lal started across the platform through the passengers, smiling and rubbing a knife and fork in his hands, to receive the food. As he reached the edge of the platform and bent forward, Ivor and Roger exchanged a glance, each took an imperceptible step forward and thrust a foot under Lal's ankles. He swayed, the dishes in his hands, and crashed over, hitting his head on the rail; curry erupted and engulfed him. He sat up and half turned, scalding juice running down his hair, tomatoes, ladyfingers, yellow rice slipping down his face, and fell back, a knife sticking out of his striped waistcoat. Ivor and Roger were among the first to jump down. The tearful boy was sent to phone for an ambulance.

'Heh heh heh.'

The old boys couldn't see the knife, and laughed away their humiliations in the café.

Lal now lay on the pile of empty mail sacks on the platform. It occurred to nobody that it wasn't an accident. The ambulance klaxon overtook the sound of the approaching train.

The incident made the evening paper; a small paragraph on the front page under the banner headline proclaiming a return to work by the railmen after the personal intervention of the Prime Minister. It seemed that Lal was comfortable in hospital with burns and a punctured lung.

Ivor rolled uneasily all night in bed, behind the window which still bore an orange shred from the last election; the quisling of the station snack bar; all his principles slithering with scalding curry down Lal's surprised face. If he could become completely evil he could forget all this, or laugh at it, continue his affair with Heather from the office, or a succession of women, refuse to attend Family Service, neglect the garden, drink himself to death, then everybody would be sorry. Would he have to use another station?

He practised a sneer on his changed face as he shaved, but the eyes in the mirror had a puffy frightened look.

'Bye dear, have a good day,' he said as he left.

An incomprehensible curse seemed to batter against the front door as he banged it. He sensed something in the atmosphere as soon as he and Roger arrived at Chubleigh station.

'Deny everything,' he muttered as they squared their shoulders, the wooden floor of the booking hall resounding hollowly like the hearts in their chests. The young porter, promoted, inspected their seasons. A knot of people was down the platform, by the far seat, obviously holding some sort of conference. Roger's elbow caught Ivor painfully on the muscle of his arm. They stopped and glanced frantically back at the booking hall, but people blocked the entrance.

'Wait for the 9.12?' said Roger stepping back a pace. A patch of bristle under his nose denoted a shaky hand. Ivor shook his head. The cluster broke. A woman pointed at Ivor and Roger.

'A necktie party,' said Roger.

'I am completely evil,' said Ivor to himself.

His umbrella was slippery in his hand. Two students were coming down the platform towards them, his long blue jeans bent and straightened, eating up the asphalt, her skirt trailed tiny chips of grit; they heard the flap of her bare feet. The two avengers garbed in their tatty integrity moved down the platform towards them. Ivor stared at the yellow tin newspaper stand and became absorbed in a blotch of rust, dog-shaped. He scratched at it with a forefinger, to elongate its stumpy tail and a flake of rust pierced the soft skin under his nail. He stared at it. 'Your nails are so neat,' Heather had said, 'just like haricot beans.'

He felt detached pity for those polished beans, as if they were to be violated in some inquisition or boiled for soup. Meanwhile Roger was finding it necessary to search his briefcase, and not unexpectedly found only *The Guardian* within, and squinted at its sideways folded print.

'About the accident yesterday –'

'Look here,' Roger started to say, but Ivor caught his sleeve.

'We're getting up a collection for Lal's family from the regulars.'

A balloon burst in Ivor's chest, suffusing his veins and face with warm liquid. His leather wallet leaped to his hand and he was stuffing a fiver into the jagged slit of the improvised collection tin, round which was pasted a piece of white paper with the simple message FOR LAL, which the girl held out.

'Turrific,' she uttered.

The male student scowled in silent accusation of ostentation. Roger managed fifty pence, which landed dully on Ivor's note.

'Right,' said the student, taking the tin and giving it a shake, and they moved on to the next passengers.

Roger and Ivor sat at opposite ends of the compartment, as if each thought the other had behaved rather badly.

The following morning the students were waiting. The boy hovered over them, his jeans seemed to sway with self-effacement.

'Personally I think the little old lady who gave 20p out of her pension should take it, but Maggie,' who had her hair in stubby pigtails today, 'seems to think you genuinely love the guy, so here you are. From us all.'

He thrust the heavy tin at Ivor, who stared up at him hopelessly.

'Give him the address, Maggie.'

She gave him a piece of paper. As if divesting themselves of a necessary but distasteful contact with the spoils of capitalism, they loped off.

'Pompous, sentimental, young twit,' said Roger.

Ivor, who had the tin, said nothing.

'You'd better go tonight,' suggested Roger. 'Get it over with.'

'Yes, we will,' said Ivor rolling the weighty embarrassing tin into his briefcase.

They met in a bar at Waterloo and fortified themselves for their task; from his seat under the red and yellow lights, above the platform, Ivor watched all the lucky commuters going home; all the fortunates who didn't have to take a tin of money to the wife and children of a man they had pushed onto the railway line for no reason.

'The more one thinks about it, the more impossible the whole thing becomes,' said Roger.

Ivor grunted. Roger went to telephone Martha.

'That's settled then,' he said as he came back.

'Same again?'

It struck Ivor that Roger was looking forward to the

evening with cheerful or morbid curiosity. He almost told him to go home, but the thought of facing Lal's wife alone was worse.

'No thanks,' he said standing up. 'The woman will be busy putting the kids to bed, maybe after visiting the hospital, we don't want to turn up stinking of booze.'

Roger sighed and followed him out. It transpired, however, that they had twenty minutes to wait for a train, and they returned to the bar. Marian had hung up on him when he telephoned; too late he remembered that it was madrigal night.

Croydon was golden when they left its station. They hired one of the taxis blazing in the forecourt and gave the driver Lal's address. The street turned out to be a long hill of terraced houses, which the taxi climbed slowly looking at the numbers.

'Bet it's that one.' Roger leaned forward and pointed at a blue-painted house with its brickwork picked out in pink, and windows and door, with hanging baskets of plastic flowers, pale green.

'They go in for that sort of thing. Really lowers the tone.'

It was at none of the picked-out houses that the taxi finally drew up. Lal's house was a discreet cream, with only a wreath of stucco leaves above the door painted dark green and a laburnum tree trailing leaves and pods over the gate, with the name 'The Laburnums'.

Ivor was fumbling with the lock of his briefcase as Roger knocked. A plump dark boy in school trousers opened the door.

'Does Mr Kharma live here?'

'My dad isn't here.'

A voice called something foreign from within. The boy answered in the same language, keeping his lustrous eyes on the two strangers, standing on a hectic yellow-orange carpet which swirled up the staircase behind him like a colony of snakes. The hall glittered with dark eyes from behind doors and the spaces of the bannisters.

'Are you from the newspaper?' asked the boy.

'No, we –'

A woman came from somewhere at the back of the house and stood behind the boy. Ivor thrust the tin at her over his head.

'On behalf of the regulars at Chubleigh Station, we'd like you to accept this small token. We were all very sorry about your husband's accident. He was very popular.'

He spoke slowly and loudly, feeling a flush seep up his neck from his collar. She stared at him almost with hostility. A smell of cooking came from the kitchen. The boy seemed to translate.

'Her eyes are like pansies, those dark velvety pansies,' thought Ivor.

'My mother says please come inside.'

'Well, that's awfully kind of you, but we really mustn't impose,' began Ivor.

'Please.'

The women and children moved back, the boy held the door wide.

'Well, just for a minute.'

Ivor and Roger stepped in. They were led into the front

room and told to sit on a black leatherette sofa backed with red, encrusted with gold thread, embossed by a bright picture of a Bengal tiger. Bamboo pictures hung on the walls and coloured brass ornaments stood on the mantelpiece and windowsill. Roger shifted his feet on the blue carpet.

'Have you seen your dad? How is he getting on? That was a rotten thing to happen.'

'He can talk now. His burns pain him. Did you see the accident?' answered the boy.

'Yes we were right there. We did what we could.'

The woman interposed a question to her son.

'Is one of you Mr Ivor and Mr Roger?' asked the boy.

'No,' said Ivor at once, but Roger was saying heartily, 'That's us. Great pals of your dad, we are.'

This was translated with some vehemence.

'All is lost,' thought Ivor. He wanted to run.

Three little girls came and sat opposite them, two on chairs and one on the arm, swinging an impossibly thin brown leg and foot in a rubber flip-flop. Lal's wife said something to the boy and went out of the room. Ivor tried to remember if there was a telephone in the hall. He placed the tin, FOR LAL, on the little carved table covered with a silk cloth, beside a Monopoly game.

'My mother says please wait. She is getting you some food. She is very grateful to you.'

The men exchanged a helpless glance. Ivor wondered if the plump boy was teased at school, and if his own children could cope so well with a second language. He was not really like a child, rather a small self-contained man in his white shirt, with sleeves turned back to show a heavy gold watch on his wrist. He seemed not to have inherited his father's jocularity; rather his mother's gloom. But of course they had something to be gloomy about, Ivor reminded himself.

The mother called from the kitchen and one of the girls left the room.

'Lovely kids,' muttered Roger. 'Beautiful eyes.'

'I don't like the way they're staring at us. I think they know. Let's get out.'

'Can't. Look worse.'

He raised his voice to the little girls. 'Do you speak English?'

'Yes.'

'Jolly good.'

The tallest girl returned with two thin conical glasses on a brass tray. Her hair was tied back in a long plait like her mother's and she had tiny gold stars in her ears.

'Would you like a drink?'

'I say, thank you very much.'

The two assassins each lifted a glass and put their lips to the thick sweet liquor.

'Cheers.'

'Cheers,' said the girl, unsmiling. She held the tray behind her back; there was nowhere to put the glasses, so they drained them. She held out the tray and went out again. The younger girls were whispering and stopped when they caught Ivor's eye. He wished someone would turn on the television or the transistor with which Lal had cheered up his customers.

'Please tell your mother she mustn't go to any trouble on our account,' he told the boy.

'She wants to repay your kindness.'

'Mustn't offend Eastern hospitality,' mumbled Roger, 'besides, I could do with some nosh. Wonder what it'll be? Smells good.'

The girl returned with the filigree glasses refilled. This time Ivor took a sip and set his glass on the floor.

'Good stuff,' said Roger, a little thickly.

'Don't know how it mixes with Scotch though.'

The mother called again from the kitchen. The little girls opened a drawer in the sideboard and took cones of incense and stood them in little brass hands and lit them. Ivor thought he heard the front door click. He reached down for his glass, the fragile stem swayed in his hand and slopped the liquor onto the floor. A child ran for a cloth and the oldest girl took his glass and brought it back brimming.

'Very clean,' remarked Roger, jerking his head at the floor.

'Is your house dirty then?' retorted the child.

'Touché,' he laughed.

'Would you like to come through,' said the boy politely. 'I'll show you the bathroom first, if you'd like to wash.'

The strange drink and heavy incense swirled round in Ivor's head, he had to put his hand to the wall as he followed the children. Fresh soap and towels seemed to have been put out in the bathroom; he glanced back as he left to make sure he had left it tidy.

'Did you put the towels back?' he whispered to Roger.

'What?' He pushed past him into the kitchen. There, Ivor felt suddenly gross among these small people as he hovered at the table and sat down clumsily on the indicated chair.

'Aren't you having any?'

'We have eaten earlier, before the hospital,' explained their little host.

Bowls of steaming rice and dishes of food smelling, to Ivor, of every spice of the orient were placed before them. The family grouped round the kitchen to watch the Englishmen eat. Incense was burning here too, the air was thick with it, sweet and acrid scents mingling.

'Please eat,' said the girl. Lal's wife drew out a chair and sat down at the opposite end of the table from Ivor. He heaped his plate until it was swimming with beautiful coloured vegetables and marbled with red and yellow juices. A full glass stood by his plate.

'It's great, it's delicious. I don't know what it is but it's great!' Roger said.

There was no need to translate this; his spoon was already digging again into a dish.

'Have some more ladyfingers, Ive.'

He scooped a heap of the little pods onto Ivor's plate and took another drink.

'Everything's all right,' thought Ivor, as he bit into the delicious ladyfingers, he straightened his shoulders which were stiff with tension, and relaxed in his chair.

'I am totally evil,' he thought, and sniggered a little at himself.

Roger put down his spoon and fork.

'D'you know,' he said, spitting rice, 'D'you know, if every immigrant family in this country was to ask one English family into their homes, just one each, for a meal like this, it would put an end to racial prejudice at one stroke. Eh, Mrs Lal? What do you say to that? I call you Mrs Lal,' he explained, 'because you people put your surnames first.'

Ivor was terrified again. If Roger was drunk would they ever escape those velvet eyes and glittering earrings, fusing, shifting, miniature watchful Lal faces, dark and golden?

'We Anglo-Saxons are a funny lot.' Roger was leaning over the table. 'We're very reserved, but if you people would just take the initiative, not be so stand-offish, you know? We can be very nice when you get to know us, can't we Ivor?'

'For God's sake, Roger!' Surely Indians were teetotal?

'Now some people think, and I know they're wrong, that your lot are a bit stuck-up, you know, toffee-nosed, unwilling to adopt our customs, living in the past. You spread the word, Mrs Lal, you give us an inch and we'll take a yard.'

He stopped suddenly and resumed shovelling. No one spoke. Ivor kept his eyes on his plate; if he stopped eating his head might crash forward into the curry; like Lal's. He blew his nose.

Roger was waving a fork at the boy; his mouth opening and shutting, trying to get the right words out. He lurched up and put his arms round two of the girls, pulling them together so that they almost kissed. The boy stepped forward to protect his sisters. Roger released them.

'These kids. Our kids. It's up to them. They're the generation that counts. You and me, Ivor, we've had our chance. They're the last chance this rotten old world's got.'

He began to cry and sat down, spooning food now into his wet mouth, now down his tie. Ivor's whole head broke into bubbles of sweat; he blotted it with his handkerchief, and saw runnels under Roger's nose . He loosened his tie. He made an effort to salvage the evening and their honour.

'How did your husband seem, Mrs Lal? In himself, I mean.' He said very slowly and courteously.

'He is as well as can be expected,' said the boy.

'Good. Good.' Ivor nodded solemnly. His eyes were caught by Mrs Kharma's; the pansies seemed drenched with dew; he had to shake his head to shift the image of himself unwrapping the gauzy sari, like the cellophane round a flower, to reveal the dark orchid within. He thought one of the little brass incense burners clenched and unclenched and almost felt the metal fingers on his throat. He kicked Roger and stood up.

'Mrs Lal, my friend and I would like to thank you for a most excellent meal. We mustn't take up any more of your precious time.'

He hauled Roger to his feet.

'It has been a privilege to meet Dad's friends. Please convey our thanks to all the kind people who contributed. But there is more to come.'

One of the girls was taking from the fridge aluminium shells of ice cream pitted with green chips of pistachio. Roger made a clumsy move towards the table. Now or never. Ivor got him into the hall.

'Mrs Lal, I want you to know,' he heard himself saying, 'I want you to know you can count on me, as a friend of your husband. He's a good man, and I'm proud to be his friend –'

'So long Gunga Din.' Roger was ruffling the boy's hair as the front door nearly clipped his fingers.

'Gloomy lot, never smiled once,' he said. 'Did you notice? No sense of humour.'

He tangled with the laburnum.

'More like some weird ritual than a meal.'

'At least one of us kept his dignity,' replied Ivor.

Ivor woke, clawing his chest as if wrenching out a knife; his pyjamas were sodden. He had a terrible pain; he was about to be sick. He bumped through in the dark, gagging himself with his hand, biting his palm, whooshing and whooping into the bowl, a burning poisonous volcano. At last he lay back on the floor, pressing his forehead on the cold tiles, then doubled up and vomited again where he lay.

'Are you all right?' came Marian's annoyed voice from the bedroom.

Spasm after spasm racked him; it was pouring from his mouth, down his nose, and when there was nothing left his stomach still heaved towards his raw throat. His insides felt sore and pink and mangled.

'Ivor?' She had forced herself out of bed.

'Go away,' he groaned. 'Just go away,' trying to pull the door shut with his foot. She took one look, and fled to be sick in the sink.

'O God, O God, I'm dying, let me die, I can't bear it. Let me die,' a voice was groaning over and over. He lay sweating and shivering for a long time. Then he pulled a towel over himself like a blanket and half dozed in the appalling smell. An iron band was screwed round his head.

Some time later he pulled himself, frozen, to his feet and set about cleaning up the fouled bathroom with newspaper and disinfectant and Ajax, washing its walls and floors and the interstices of the hot water pipes, specked and freckled with his guilt. Every time he bent, the burning vice tightened on his skull and his teeth clattered uncontrollably. He put his pyjamas in the dirty linen basket for Marian to wash. He stood in a towel at the open window, watching the strange sky lighten over the heavy oaks. The telephone drilled.

Martha Henry's frantic voice battered against his caved-in chest. He couldn't bear to put the receiver to his ear.

'He won't die,' he said, and put the phone down.

Sitting on the bath's edge, watching it fill, steam flowering up the turquoise sides, in the sour aftermath, and the draught from the open window, he thought: 'You've got to hand it to them. Not a word of the pain we caused them. Not a flicker of emotion. Just a silent revenge. You've got to respect them for that.'

The Late Wasp

'Well, we've got a super day for it, Darren.'

'Yes, sir,' replied Cheeseman miserably.

They set off across the asphalt to run the gauntlet of the classroom windows. Mr Glenn with his rucksack, a huge orange edifice bristling with buckles and straps, inherited from his father, bouncing on his back, and Cheeseman with a Tesco carrier bag trying to hide itself against his leg.

As they passed the sixth form common-room a girl, lying languorously half out of the window, called to some-one inside.

'Glenda's wearing shorts.'

Her friend appeared beside her to watch Mr Glenn stride past on white legs that might have survived a fusillade of paprika, his peppery beard at a defiant angle.

'The saddest story every told.'

She drew deeply on a sweet cigarette and passed across a crumpled paper bag of rhubarb and custards, striped pink and yellow lozenges, provoking memories of school puddings of yesteryear before the canteen was turned into a cafeteria. The girls were due to leave school in a few days and, overcome by nostalgia for their youth, were feeding it on childish sweets and reducing the insides of their mouths to exquisitely agonising sponges with bittersweet crystals and shards of sugar. Such was their hyperaesthesia that a shoe bag on a peg or a first-year child with name-tapes on the outsides of its socks could reduce them to tears despite, or because of, the poignant knowledge that soon all this would mean nothing to them. The common-room ashtrays were spangled heaps of glossy wrappers, lollipop sticks, spent cartridges of sherbet fountains.

'Where are they going?'

'Why are we here? Where do we come from? Where are we going?' replied her friend closing the window.

Mr Glenn and Darren Cheeseman were setting off on a Ramble on the Downs. As they crossed the tennis courts a low volley –

'Cheesey's wearing a Harrington' – smacked into the back of Darren's head.

'He can't be' – struck his ear as he turned.

'Why not?' – thud.

'Nobody wears Harringtons any more' – caught him full in the face.

Mr Glenn seemed unaware of this rally which had left dull red marks on Darren's face under his glasses, or of the rude sign which he made behind his back. He was staring, as Darren was now, at the glittering coaches, parked at the gates, into which Mrs Nihill, French, was counting with a clipboard the rest of the second year; girls in short vivid skirts, boys and girls with hair spiked into crests and cockades with school soap, like an officious florist bundling heaps of dahlias into a refrigerated vehicle, for export to Boulogne. On the steps of the second coach Bob Drumbell, PE, rested for a moment, his brutish hand on the sparkling Bermudas of Hannah Guilfoyle, History, as she climbed aboard.

'It's not fair,' thought Cheeseman.

'It's not fair,' thought Mr Glenn.

If it was anybody's fault that they were standing, in silence, together at the bus-stop that was the starting point of their outing, it was Cheeseman's. A form had been issued to each child in the second year proposing a day of Educational Visits and giving a choice of four; Boulogne, Brighton, Bodiam Castle at varying prices, and a Ramble on the Downs, free. Everybody except Darren Cheeseman, a new boy who had failed to settle, had signed up for the trip to Boulogne.

'Its quite encouraging, isn't it, that little Cheeseman has opted for the ramble?' Mr Glenn, Geography, a new boy himself, had said in the staffroom. 'Perhaps at last we've hit on something that interests him.'

Mrs Nihill snorted. She prided herself on her work on the pastoral side.

'I very much doubt if that's the case. Lives in two rooms with his Dad on the Belmont Estate – Mum's done a bunk, Dad's out of work . . .' she boasted, giving a Gallic shrug and brushing a crumb of Ryvita from her crimplene knee. Quelle know-all. No doubt already in her imagination she was heaving her haunches round the *hypermarché* behind a heaped trolley. At her accusation of greenness Mr Glenn felt his face turn red and buried it in his World Wildlife

Fund mug. When he raised it he realised that he had been elected in a silent ballot to accompany Cheeseman to the Downs. Hannah Guilfoyle, far from showing disappointment that he would not be going to Boulogne, had laughed at his plight. In fact it was probably she who had proposed him.

Cheeseman, alone in the library at lunchtime, spotted his approach from the window.

'Darren, if it's a question of money . . . I'm sure something could be arranged – the school has a fund. . . .'

'What money? Look, sir,' he pointed to a picture in the book he was reading. 'Did you know that the chalk blue butterfly is occasionally found in albino form? Do you think we'll see one on our ramble?'

As the library door closed behind Mr Glenn, Cheeseman pulled out a comic from beneath the book and resumed reading: 'Dear Cathy and Claire, Please help me. Although I am only thirteen my. . . .'

'Here comes the bus,' Mr Glenn was able to say at last. He paid the fares and followed Darren to the back seat. At each stop ancients mounted slowly with their shopping bags. If buses travelled by bus, Mr Glenn reflected, this one would take ten minutes to heave its wheels up the steps, turn to greet its cronies, have a joke with the driver, then fumble in a pocket somewhere in its metal side for its senior citizens' bus-pass. Mr Glenn glanced round, apart from Darren he was the youngest passenger by some forty years. So old and yet they all seemed to have so much still to say. He wondered why the driver did not turn round and roar, 'Silence!' and was disturbed by an image of a playground full of grey- and white-haired children leap-frogging and kicking footballs and turning skipping ropes.

He was shamed into moving his rucksack from the luggage space to make room for two shopping trolleys, beldams in faded tartan, which lurched together as the bus, meeting another in the narrow lane, had to reverse with a great scraping of twigs on the windows; and the two green gaffers hooted at each other as they passed.

It was as he was sitting down again that he saw someone enter the bus without paying his fare; elegant, narrow-waisted in black and yellow stripes. He came in by the window, and it might cost him his life. He sat unnoticed on the glass. Mr Glenn squirmed. He saw himself rise and lunge down the aisle on his freckled legs, scoop up the wasp in his handkerchief and flap it out of the window. His face grew red, his bare skin sweated on the prickly seat, as he braced himself for ridicule.

'Wasps are early this year,' he heard.

'I had two in my kitchen yesterday.'

The wasp moved tantalisingly to the rim of the window. 'Now,' said Mr Glenn to himself. 'Quickly. Don't be such a great wet Glenn, just get up and do it. You know you should.' He willed it to crawl over the edge into the air. It sat and he sat. Beside him Cheeseman was rustling about in his carrier bag. He pulled out a can and ripped it open; a few sticky drops fell onto Mr Glenn's thigh.

'Want a drink, sir?'

'No,' said Mr Glenn sharply. 'Put it away.'

The wasp zoomed down the zone of the scent. A flat cap snatched from a head whipped it to the floor, a blunt toe squelched it. The early wasp was the late wasp. Mr Glenn stared out of the window trying to think that it did not matter that something beautiful was broken; that something which should have been alive was dead.

The bus rumbled on like an old tuneless wurlitzer while the driver gave a virtuoso demonstration of its revs and groans and wheezes at every bend and hill. So that when Mr Glenn and Cheeseman at last disengaged themselves and the rucksack, they stood on the grass verge with slight headaches, stunned by silence as the bus's green backside wobbled away in a cloud of heat haze and exhaust.

'This way, I think. Over the level crossing and up that field and then onto the hills.'

Mr Glenn looked up at the exposed surface of chalk. He saw it as a bride and the path that led up to it as her glittering train. He didn't offer this conceit to Cheeseman as he followed him onto the level crossing. On either side of them the flashing rails raced away into the past or future. Glenn stood with a sense of being no one and nowhere, stranded in eternity on the wooden island.

'Come on, sir!'

'Yes, yes. Thank you Darren.' He stumbled gratefully onto the path where thistleheads flared among the glittering dust and stones.

'You feeling OK?'

'Yes, I'm fine thanks. I just felt a bit funny there for a moment – I didn't have time for any breakfast – I was a bit late getting up.'

He felt his rucksack, which contained his lunch and a copy of *Cities of The Plain*, Part I, pat him encouragingly on the back for almost achieving a conversation. He looked round for something to say to consolidate his success.

'Look,' he cried, pointing into the blue.

'That bird – isn't it a kawk or a hestrel – oh, dear, you've missed it.'

'Which do you think it was, sir?'

'I'm not sure. Definitely some sort of bird of prey. I expect you'd have been able to identify it.'

Darren didn't respond to the flattery; he pulled a long piece of grass and stuck it in his mouth, chewed irritably, wrenched it out, threw it away and pulled another.

'Do you smoke, sir?' he spat.

'No, I don't. Why? And there's no need to call me sir today; after all we're here to enjoy ourselves.'

'Oh, really?'

Mr Glenn hoped he had misheard, but unease started to churn away again. They were now on a track evidently used by cows, balancing on the edges of deep ruts whose thick clods of dried mud crumbled like stale gingerbread under Mr Glenn's boots and pierced the soles and sides of Darren's plimsolls. Mr Glenn cleared his throat.

'Why don't you put your bag in my rucksack, then you'll have your hands free?'

'Sokay.'

'No, go on.'

Mr Glenn crouched down on the mud offering his buckles. He squatted there until his knees cracked and sweat dripped into his eyes, feeling like a foolish frog on a dried-up river bed, fearing that Darren had sneaked away, or was going to kick him.

'Darren?'

At last he felt the straps being lifted and the carrier bag falling into the rucksack.

'Mind my thermos!'

As he straightened up he fell forward on his hands and knees. He brushed a bead of blood from his knee, which was jolly painful, a bit of grit must have got embedded, and looked at Darren for some concerned query. He saw him wipe a smirk from his mouth with the back of his hand. As schoolmaster he should have felt gratified to see a pupil taking literally that often-repeated command – 'and you can wipe that silly grin off your face!' As it was he decided to risk septicaemia rather than take out his first-aid kit.

Darren seemed inclined to lounge and flop on every fence post and tree stump.

'Is it much further, sir?'

'Is what much further?'

'This place where we're going to.'

'We're not going anywhere in particular. This is supposed to be a Ramble. We just ramble around and observe the wild life and flora. . . .'

'Who's she?'

Mr Glenn heaving a pedagogic sigh, exhaled panic and the knowledge that he would disappoint as he bowed his head to enter a green tunnel which led uphill through a little wood.

'A green thought in a green shade . . .,' he said.

'No answer came the loud reply,' he added silently,

holding a bramble to stop it from whipping across Darren's face, and having done this once, felt obliged to hold back every branch, bramble, briar, nettle that he encountered. Unspoken words jumbled about in his head like plastic fragments in a broken kaleidoscope. From time to time he cleared his throat. Suddenly Darren had to stop short to avoid falling over Mr Glenn's haunches, as he sank to his knees and seemed to be adoring something.

'Fly agaric,' he breathed, turning a face flushed with pleasure to the boy's.

Darren looked. A sort of half-eaten toadstool, curled up at the edges, red with white blotches.

'Is it poison?'

'Yes, it is. Very.'

'Deadly poison?'

'It could be. Don't kick it.'

'It was mouldy anyway. Do you think we'll find any Death Caps?'

'No.'

After a few more minutes' silent trudging Mr Glenn pointed to swags and garlands of green berries tinged with yellow looping the trees.

'Just imagine what it will be like in the autumn, the whole wood decked with necklaces of scarlet beads. This is white bryony, isn't it? I think it's black bryony that has the heart-shaped leaves. . . .'

'Are they poison?'

'Really Darren, anyone would think you intended to poison the whole school!'

He laughed uneasily when Darren did not reply and

added quickly, 'Those black berries are dogwood. They used to make arrows from it in the olden days.'

'How could they make arrows from berries, sir?' Mr Glenn sneaked a look at his watch. He reckoned lunch could be spun out for three-quarters of an hour, if he ate very slowly.

'Do you like them old-fashioned watches, sir? I've got a digital watch at home.'

'Really. What's that you've found? Something interesting?' he said eagerly.

'Looks like an old pair of tights. Wonder how they got there?'

'I haven't the faintest idea,' he blushed.

Darren was waving them about on the end of a stick.

'Funny place to leave a pair of tights.'

'Do throw them away and come along!'

Mr Glenn was anxious lest Darren root up something worse. Darren flung the tights into the air; they caught on a branch where they hung dangling – obscene and sinister empty legs.

'There's a little plateau just ahead where we can stop to have our lunch. I don't know about you, but I'm starving.'

'I found a corset in a car park once, in Croydon.'

'I say, a Roman snail!' Mr Glenn bent gratefully over this piece of wildlife which sat obligingly in their path.

'Revolting.'

'Oh, I think he's rather magnificent.'

They stared at the moist granular body under the creamy swirls of shell, the glistening knobs on the ends of the horns, a tiny green leaf disappearing into its mouth.

'Revolting eating snails, I mean, I couldn't, could you, sir? I bet that's what they're doing now – eating snails and frogs' legs, and getting drunk, I bet, knocking back the old vino.'

Jealous venom frothed like garlic butter through Darren's teeth. He leaped at a liana hanging from an ancient honeysuckle.

'I bet Miss Guilfoyle enjoys a drink, don't you, sir? And Mr Dumbrell.'

He swung gibbering four inches from the ground, his glasses lewd blank disks of malice.

Mr Glenn's shorts crushed out a sharp scent of thyme as he sat down, the warm grass tickled his legs pleasantly. Behind them rose the chalk face, now more like a wedding cake with green icing than a bride and below them the valley: river, church spire, village and fields and beyond them the town.

'Magnificent view.'

'It's a bit, well, rural, innit?' said Darren critically.

'For goodness sake, Cheeseman. Mind where you put your feet – you're treading on a harebell. You wanted to come on this flaming ramble.'

He reached for his rucksack, his hands shaking with anger.

'Did I?'

When Darren had realised that no one else had signed on for the ramble, pride had not allowed him to admit that he did not want to go, or to apply to the school for financial help towards the trip to Boulogne on which he wanted passionately to go; it would have been pointless to ask his father for the money. He had intended not to turn up at school that morning and spend the day wandering round the town, eat his lunch in the rec., perhaps do a little shoplifting; but as ill-luck would have it, his father, on his way to buy cigarettes, had walked him to the bus-stop and several of his classmates had been on the bus. So here he was stuck half way up a hill with this berk in shorts bleating about harebells.

'I don't believe it. I do not believe it.' Mr Glenn was scrabbling in his rucksack; out came Proust, out came a thermos flask, out came a first-aid kit, out came Darren's carrier bag.

'I seem to have forgotten my lunch,' he had to admit at last, handing Darren his.

A forlorn tableau of bran rolls bulging with salad, yogurt, two apples, one red, one green and a bar of chocolate floated before his eyes. He licked his chops as he watched Darren bite into an oblong of white bread. He unscrewed his thermos, and poured a stream of clear hot water into the cup; he had forgotten to put in the tea. After a few minutes he moved closer to Darren.

'That looks tasty.'

Darren pushed the bag towards him.

'May I? That's awfully kind. What's in them?'

'Those are ketchup, and those are ketchup and salad cream.'

'Super,' said Mr Glenn faintly. As he sank his teeth into

the flaccid, oozing bread, he noticed a little blue dot of mould on the crust.

'Can I offer you a little hot water in exchange?' he asked hoping for another sandwich.

'S'all right, thanks, I've got some shandy,' said Darren and drank it. Mr Glenn watched him pour the last few drops onto the grass as he sipped his water.

Darren stood up. 'See you in a minute,' he said.

'Right. Don't get lost.'

Mr Glenn went in the opposite direction. When he returned Darren was not back. He stole a sandwich and lay back luxuriating in Darren's absence and watched a bee rummaging in a knapweed's rough purple wheel and took up his book to avoid the memory of a wasp.

The shadow of a cloud fell on his page; he looked up expecting to see white sails on the sea at Balbec and was surprised to find himself on grass not sand, and realised that Darren had not returned and jumped up and pushed his way through the wayfaring trees into which the boy had disappeared. Little tracks ran in all directions. He whirled like a demented humming top, seeing Darren lying at the bottom of a crevasse, then launched himself forward, fighting twigs and brambles. Suddenly he heard very faint music ahead and burst through the bushes, half expecting to come upon Pan or some satyr or faun piping in the glade.

Darren lay stretched at ease, his head against a white rock, his eyes closed, a corkscrew of smoke spiralling into the blue from a cigarette between the fingers of one languid hand, while the other beat time to the music of a tiny radio. Mr Glenn, calcified with rage, the frustrations of the morning whirling like furies in his brain, stood and stared. Then he tiptoed towards the erstwhile faun.

'I say!'

As he turned at the shout something heavy hurled itself at his shins and he felt a sharp pain in the seat of his shorts; he howled and danced clutching his torn shorts and rubbing his bruised, perhaps broken, legs. Two golden retrievers leaped round him barking, clawing his chest and arms, thrusting hard yellow heads into his face, while he flailed feebly at them and Darren sat laughing.

'Cindy! Bella! Down!'

With a last snap they writhed in a yellow heap at his feet. Two navy blue figures in denim skirts and T-shirts were sliding down the chalk towards them.

'Do you know this man?' one demanded of Darren, who was fondling a dog.

'Madam, do you take me for a denizen of Gomorrah?' said Mr Glenn.

'I beg your pardon?' She bristled at a suspected insult.

'Do you know this man?' repeated her friend.

Mr Glenn waited for Darren to say, 'I've never seen him before in my life.'

'Tell her, Darren.'

At last Cheeseman looked up from tying the dog's ears in a bow on top of its head.

'He's my teacher,' he said. 'Mr Glenn. Whitcombe School.'

'Well, if you're sure. . . .'

'Funny sort of teacher, encouraging a child to smoke. . . .'

'Oh, that's the sort of thing they teach them at school these days, didn't you know? They're all Marxists and sociologists. . . .'

'We're on a nature ramble,' said Mr Glenn with dignity, backing away with his hand on his shorts.

'Come along, Darren. We're going to look for fossils.'

Darren was reluctant to leave the dogs.

'Who's a good boy then? Good dog! Aren't they nice dogs, sir?'

'Bitches,' corrected his teacher loudly.

'We had a dog once,' began Darren conversationally, 'but he had to. . . .'

'Shut up, you little creep, and walk in front of me.'

'This looks a likely place,' he said stopping at the foot of a glossy glacier of chalk. 'Let's have a nose round here.' The chalk felt dry and silky under their feet. 'Don't go too high.'

'Found one!' shouted Darren at once.

'Let's have a look. No, I'm afraid not,' he had to add, reluctant to disappoint.

'What about this one then?' holding up an equally undistinguished lump of chalk.

'I don't think so. Have another look.'

Darren hurled his stone at the cliff face causing a small avalanche. Mr Glenn grubbed silently. Black clouds smudged the sun.

'I say, Darren! I think I've – yes, it is – it's part of an ammonite!' He looked round. Some thirty feet above him, clinging to the stump of a scrubby bush, was Darren.

'Come down at once,' he croaked.

Darren turned and waved, then gripped again the bending stem; a stream of stones trickled from each foot. He scrabbled up a little higher resting one foot against the bush.

'Darren! Come down. It's dangerous! If you don't come down at once I'm putting you in Detention!'

Darren inched upwards.

'Right! You're in Detention!' His voice rose to a squeak. He felt his own feet tingle, his knees wobbled and he felt the ground sway as he looked upwards. He shook his head hard and the landscape righted itself. Darren had not moved. There was nothing above him to grasp.

'Are you stuck?'

Darren, crouched on the chalk face, was paralysed and dumb.

Glenn looked round wildly – the navy-blue ladies – anybody; only a useless black crow flapping wildly into a black bush high above.

'Hold on. I'm coming up –' he had to shout. Despite his stout socks and boots Mr Glenn suffered acutely if he had to stand on a chair to change a light bulb. . . . He set off on all fours up the scree, keeping his eyes fixed on white stones, with plants too shallow-rooted to grasp, his shirt stuck to his back, slowly, slowly, toe-holds crumbling under his boots. A fine drizzle glazed the chalk, little lumps slipped under his fingers.

'It's all a question of momentum,' he muttered. 'Just keep going forward, don't stop, don't look down.'

A little rock hit him on the forehead and then Darren hurtled past screaming. Glenn snatched at him and caught his sleeve; his fingers tightened on the bone in the skinny arm; he took his whole weight in one hand and pulled him up beside him, to hold him in so close an embrace that he saw a smudge of dried salad cream fringing his lip. Instinctively, he put up his hand to wipe his own mouth, lost his grip on the chalk and started to slide. Darren tried to pull him back but was dragged down himself. The radio fell from Darren's pocket and bounced down the stones. Teacher and pupil, a tangle of arms and legs, slithered, a grotesque terrified spider, after it. Glenn, catching a tuft of tough grass, dared look down; they were only ten feet from the ground. He guided Darren's fingers to a tiny ledge and placed his foot in a hollow. So they continued their unheroic descent.

At the foot Glenn sat down heavily on a heap of stones, his arms round his shuddering legs. Between his boots he saw the cracked blue case of Darren's radio; he picked it up; a battery rolled away.

'I'm afraid it's broken.'

Darren snatched it, then threw it down and stamped on it, grinding the plastic and blue and orange wires into the chalk.

'Don't matter,' he said. 'It's only a cheap old thing. I've gotta Walkman at home.'

'Like your digital watch,' thought Mr Glenn.

As they sat on the bus Mr Glenn, his knees still shaking, gloomily composed tomorrow's essay: 'A Ramble on the Downs', Darren Cheeseman, 2G.

'The best bit about the ramble was when I found a pair of old tights. Mr Glenn got bit on the bum by a dog, then I got stuck up a cliff and my radio got smashed. Then we went home. Tired but happy at the end of a perfect day.'

They stood on the drizzly pavement looking at each other, the two wets, chalk-stained, damp, grazed, bleeding in their ruined clothes.

'There's no point in going back to school now,' said Mr Glenn. 'We can make our separate ways home from here.'

Darren stared past him through his rainy glasses; Mr Glenn followed his gaze to the hill far away, a white cake iced in vicious green; bland, treacherous, impossibly high, but conquered. Suddenly Darren shot out an awkward fist and punched Mr Glenn lightly on the arm.

'See ya then, Glenda.'

Mr Glenn punched clumsily back.

'See ya, Cheesey.'

Family Service

'I am going to remain very calm.' Then a scream like a demon came out of her mouth.

'Is nobody in this house but me capable of putting away a cereal packet? Look at this tablecloth! There's milk and sugar all over it. And the floor! I don't know why I bother – if I come into this kitchen one more time and find the sink full of dishes, I'll – '

Helen Brigstock clamped her hand over her mouth.

'Shut up, shut up, shut up,' she told herself. Her teeth fought against her fingers; she felt a painful bite as teeth met flesh. A cannonade of church bells exploded faintly beyond the steamed up window.

Now, as when a child, Helen saw Sunday written in gold. But today how bleared and smeared and tarnished the letters. Her bulgy self, her unsatisfactory family. The sun, in a cone of dancing dust, struck grease and crumb, her distorted face reflected in the spotted kettle, highlighting every failure.

The day that had started so well had begun to go wrong when she made the mistake of stepping onto the bathroom scales as she dressed after breakfast. She would have to lose at least five pounds before Christmas and it was already the second Sunday in Advent. Scrambled egg and buttered toast weighed heavily on her as she finished dressing. If she didn't have any lunch . . . or any roast potatoes at least. . . .

The potatoes had provoked her fury. She had come down to the kitchen to prepare them so that they, and the chicken, could cook while the family was at church and just because she had left the breakfast table first everybody had decamped, leaving the kitchen in a state of unbelievable squalor and the sink full of dishes that she would have to wash before she could peel the potatoes. She heaved a sodden saucepan from the washing-up bowl. Scummy scrambled egg wrecked her nail polish as she scrubbed. She would have no time to repair it. She almost told the church bells to shut up.

She turned the hot tap on hard to drown the image of her mother, her father and herself, arms linked, walking over a frosty field to church. Then there had been time to study the crystals on a leaf or frozen spider's web; once a fox had run past them, stopped, turned back and stared them full in the face.

At last, the faceted potatoes ranged whitely round the pink chicken in the oven, Helen ran upstairs to the bedroom.

'I don't believe it! I don't believe it!' A fat ladder had sprung up her new tights leaving her leg grinning through the rungs. She tore off the tights and started raking madly through a drawer, throwing things on the floor.

The piercing notes of a recorder transfixed her, stabbing tears from her eyes as she listened. Julian, her son, in his innocent way had reminded her of what Sunday was all about. Helen stood, with pastel underwear like sugared almonds round her feet. What did clothes matter? – as long as one had some on, of course. What did it matter if she was overweight? She had so much to be grateful for, her health and strength, one should just be glad that one had enough to eat. When one thought of the starving black millions. . . . Anyway, she could easily lose five pounds by Christmas.

Helen set off along the passage to Julian's room. She would sit on his bed and say, 'Julian, I want to thank you. With your music you have just taught Mummy a valuable lesson. Oh yes, you have, darling. I know you think Mummy knows everything, but sometimes it takes a little boy to. . . .'

She tapped on, and opened, his bedroom door.

'Darling – What on earth do you think you're doing, lying on your bed, not even dressed, playing that stupid thing? Have you any idea of the time?'

Her eye caught a toy snake at the foot of the bed.

'You little reptile,' she shouted. 'You've got no con-sideration – get dressed at once! Have you forgotten that you're supposed to be reading a prayer in church or does it mean nothing to you?'

Julian had been named, secretly, after the eldest boy in the Famous Five books, a tall, well-spoken boy. This Julian, at eleven, was small for his age, and whatever they taught them at Pembury Court, and sometimes Helen wondered what it was, it certainly wasn't how to speak properly.

'Besides,' she heard her own terrible voice go on, 'that tune you were playing – if you were to read your Bible, I think you'd find that not only did Jesus never say that He was Lord of the Dance, but also that there is no record of Him ever having danced. . . .'

Mother and son, he lying on his back in pyjama trousers, recorder dangling from his lip, stared at each other until Helen dropped her eyes and slammed out of the room to fling herself with a dry sob onto her own bed, biting the duvet.

'Pull yourself together, Brigstock!' she told herself sharply. 'This won't do!'

She found a pair of intact tights and pulled them on. They came up as far as her bra.

'It doesn't matter.' So what if they should roll down making an ugly ridge at the waistband of her skirt. 'You're going to church to worship God. It doesn't matter what you look like.' When the zip of her boot caught a mouthful of plump calf in its teeth, she didn't scream, so that she felt she had got the upper hand. Standing in the bedroom doorway, she shouted:

'Girls! Are you nearly ready? We've got to leave in eight minutes!'

'No answer came the stern reply,' she said aloud, wryly. Where on earth was Roger?'

'Roger?'

No answer from her husband. Oh, honestly!

'Roger!'

'I'm in the bathroom.'

'Well, could you please hurry up! There are other people in this house besides you. Jane! Hannah! Are you two ready?'

She stumped along to Jane's room, stooping angrily from time to time to pick up pieces of fluff, thread, hair, that glared up from the red carpet. When she flung open Jane's door it was with a great gobbet, like some disgusting domestic owl's pellet, in her hand.

Jane lay face downward on her bed reading, presenting an extremely irritating pair of jeans to her mother.

'Jane, what on earth do you think you're doing?'

'I'm just having my Quiet Time.'

'Your Quiet Time! I wish I had time to have a Quiet Time! If you really think you're virtuous lying there reading the Bible while your mother washes up and peels potatoes and picks up filth from the floor – you could at least read the proper version instead of that unpoignant rubbish with its silly drawings, do you want to reduce The Greatest Story Ever Told to a strip cartoon? Well, do you? And if, if. . . .'

Again Helen wished that someone would silence it, but the dreadful voice went on.

'. . . if you've got any ideas about having "chosen the better part", forget them. I'd like to get hold of every single copy of that so-called "Good News Bible" and rip out the story of Martha and Mary. Talk about Unfair!'

Jane sat up, her fair hair falling back from her face.

'Sorry, Mum. Is there anything you'd like me to do?'

'Do? Do? Yes, you can get out the hoover and – oh,

131

forget it – it's too late. Just get ready! And couldn't you put on a pretty dress for once instead of those awful jeans?'

Jane's voice was hurt.

'You said you liked them. . . .'

'I do – it's just – oh – '

Helen stood helplessly in the doorway, the wad of fluff greasy in her sweating hand, then crashed out of the room. She collided with Roger in the passage.

'Darling?'

She pulled past without answering. She locked herself in the bathroom and collapsed on the dirty-linen basket, head in hands, rocking backwards and forwards. 'Oh God, I don't want to be like this. Please help me.'

'Mummy?'

A loud knocking on the door.

'Go away. Just go away,' she muttered.

'Mummy, are you in there?'

Helen flung open the door.

Little Hannah stood, a dramatic figure in vest and knickers.

'Mummy, it's not fair. Jane's allowed to go to church in jeans, so why can't I?'

'Not fair? Not fair?' screamed her mother. 'Is it fair that there are splashes of toothpaste all over the bathroom floor and the dirty-linen basket is full of dirty clothes that no one but I will wash and that everyone else will expect to reappear miraculously clean and ironed? Is that fair?'

Hannah fled.

Helen heard Roger rattling the car keys.

'Oh, shut up!'

She stared at herself in the mirror – pale, red eyed, her hair jumping at the comb in a mad electric mass. If only Father and Mother weren't watching. . . .

At last they were all in the car and Roger switched on the ignition. Helen turned round, deliberately calm.

'Got your prayer, Ju?'

'Yeah, it's here.' He fluttered a grey piece of paper towards her.

'Good boy. Stop the car! Roger, stop!'

'What now? He's got his prayer.'

'His nails! Get out of the car, Julian! His nails are disgusting! He's not standing up in church reading a prayer with nails like that!'

'There isn't time. We'll never get a parking space if we don't leave now.' Roger pulled out.

'If anyone ever, except me, did anything, we wouldn't have this rush every Sunday.'

'I did stack the dishes for you,' came Roger's mild voice from his complacent baggy polo-neck sweater.

'For me? For me? You make it sound as if they were all my dishes – '

'Well, actually, darling, if you remember, your mother gave them to us on our – '

'Don't you drag my mother into this!'

'No one will see Julian's nails.' Jane attempted to arbitrate.

'God will.'

The church forecourt was jammed with the cars of the

wise virgins. The Brigstocks were forced to park in a side street and arrived panting on the long path through the gravestones.

Roger put his hand on Helen's arm; she shook it off.

'Couldn't you have put on a tie? I don't subscribe to this jeans and shirt-sleeves religion. Now we'll never get a decent pew – '

'Calm down, darling.'

The peal of the bell had changed to a rapid commanding single note.

'It's the Hurry-Up Bell,' said Hannah hanging heavily on her mother's arm, who wouldn't look at her, as if it had not been she who had invented the term in the children's earliest years.

'We'll be stuck behind the choirstalls again. Julian, get off that grave, there are dead people in them, you know! Of course, if some people didn't spend three hours in the bathroom – that reminds me, I must put air freshener on my shopping list.'

'You know scrambled egg always upsets my stomach,' said Roger.

She saw that she had managed to wound him, too, at last.

'That's the thanks I get for preparing a nice family breakfast.'

'Hi.'

Sylvia, her friend, loomed up behind a mausoleum.

Helen cracked her dry face into a smile.

'Beautiful morning,' she said.

'Beautiful,' agreed Sylvia, 'if one happens to like paintings by Rowland Hilder,' and laughed as she overtook them.

Trust her. Why did she always have to try to say something clever? Helen wondered why they were friends. Anyway, surely Sylvia must have seen that Rowland Hilder snowscape with sheep a hundred times on the lounge wall? Then, suddenly cheered by the sight of her friend's immense bum swaying in peasant skirt above cowboy boots, she felt her own excess pounds fall from her, although her tights threatened to sag or bag. The frosty grass glittered, the path shone blue, the names of the dead were picked out in rhinestones and fool's gold.

She put an arm through Roger's and Julian's and pulled them to a halt.

'I'm sorry I was so ratty, darlings. It's just that – '

Hannah screamed.

On the path in front of them lay a dead blue-tit. The family stood staring down at it. It lay, tiny, frozen; blue and saffron leaking into the melting path.

'Will you bury it, Daddy?'

'There isn't time, darling.'

'We could put it in that tomb over there, look there's a hole in the side,' suggested Julian.

'Don't be so ridiculous,' snapped his mother.

Julian shrugged.

'But, Daddy.' Hannah raised tearful eyes. 'Someone might not see it and – and – walk on it!'

'Daddy told you, there isn't time! Maybe on the way out.'

'Just because you don't care about a poor little dead

135

bird. Well, I think God's cruel to let a poor little bird die in His own graveyard!'

'It's all part of His plan, darling.' Roger attempted to lift his rigid daughter, whose shoes were glued to the path. 'We can't expect to understand. He sees the meanest sparrow. . . .'

'It's a blue-tit.'

'Oh God.' Julian strode on ahead.

'I've told you not to say "God". Especially on a Sunday.'

Helen thumped her son between the shoulder blades of his school blazer, which had cost twenty-three pounds, although to look at the state of it you'd never guess. Behind her, she heard Roger's voice, infected by her, a hideous parody of her own.

'Will you stop snivelling, Hannah? Close your mouth! Did you clean your teeth this morning? They look like – like – mossy tombstones!'

'Well, I suppose everyone's forgotten that I'm supposed to be reading this bloody prayer,' said Julian as the Brigstocks entered the church and almost snatched their books from the smiling sidesman. They found a vacant pew near the back.

'Mummy, can I go and sit with – '

'Of course you can't! We'll all sit together!'

Then she realised that Jane had sloped off to sit with her friends. . . .

She slumped heavily onto her seat.

'Of course, I'm parked behind a pillar!' thought Helen. She pretended not to notice that Roger was silently offering to change places and sank her knees on the cold stone floor, the clumsily broidered hassock swinging on its hook. She waited for the familiar peace to descend. Nothing happened. Her ruined hands writhed in her gloves. She became aware of Julian shoving up against her. She opened an eye to glare at him. An old lady was mopping and mowing, in a faint scent of lavender water and mothballs, her way into the pew. Why did old ladies insist on wearing musty velour jelly-moulds on their heads? Helen sat up. The choir was coming in.

'Let us sit, or kneel, to pray.'

Typical! Typical! She assumed that it was meant as a dispensation to the aged or handicapped; but half this casual congregation found sitting the best position in which to address its God. Well, she just jolly well hoped that God would prove as easy-going at the Judgement Day! Instead of closing her eyes, Helen stared at a window. The shadow of birds' wings flickered across the stained glass and fluttered on a pillar. A bowl of forced daffodils and honesty on the sill – the stained glass, the birds – sudden tears dissolved the lump in her heart making it warm and stringy like melted mozzarella.

'We have left undone those things which we ought to have done, and we have done those things which we ought not to have done – ' said a voice in her head.

She had screamed at Julian's bare chest, which she so loved, with its pretty little bones, instead of offering him moral support when he was probably very nervous. She had shouted at him for not reading the Bible, and at Jane for reading the Bible, and at Hannah, and at Roger. . . .

Helen prayed that the prayers would go on until she was composed and had found a tissue.

'I'm sorry, Daddy,' she prayed.

The congregation came to itself. Helen concealed a sniff in the shifting of knees. She hoped that she would have a chance to repair, secretly, her face before she had to greet the vicar at the church door in the brutal Sunday sunshine.

At a given signal, Julian left her side and walked nonchalantly up the aisle. He stood at the front of the church, on the chancel steps.

'Dear God,' he began, as if reading a thank-you letter written to some obscure uncle. 'We thank you for our Homes and Families, our Mothers and Fathers.'

Helen heard no more; her eyes and ears were blocked with tears. Dimly she saw the sun streaming through stained glass tinting hair and ears ruby and emerald – Julian's ears, wonderful emerald transparent organs, his moist ruby mouth. Flesh; vulgar, beautiful – the choir sang an iridescent anthem.

The sermon came as an anticlimax. Advent. Helen tried to recapture her feelings, but they were gone, like the sun, which had disappeared, leaving the church dull and cold. Christmas – Helen heard only a panicky ripping of wrapping paper and the snickering sellotape.

'Stop sniffing,' she whispered savagely at Hannah and thrust her own wet tissue in a sodden ball into her lap.

Outside the church Helen felt pincers on her arm. She looked. The old lady who had pushed into their pew had laid a black glove on her coat sleeve.

'Such a nice little family,' she was saying. 'I see you every Sunday.'

Helen smiled. 'I do think it's important for a family to worship together,' she said.

The Brigstocks piled into the car and drove home to eat some pieces of a dead bird, which would have been browning nicely if Helen had switched on the oven.

Soft Volcano

'There is nothing like the sound of children singing hymns for deceiving us into thinking that there is some hope for mankind.'

So thought Rose Rossi as emanations of goodness came from the grey and green pullovers of the children on the virginia-creeper-wreathed, hop-entwined stage. Shrill recorders pierced the wooden rafters and played havoc with strained parents' voices and left them straying somewhere round the children's heads. The Harvest bread began to wobble and red apples were swelling and doubling their number.

Richard Garlick heard a raindrop fall on the mimeographed songsheet of the woman next to him. He looked at the window; it was closed. So far, aware of Janet on his left, he had sensed the woman on his right only as a brown velvet sleeve, a ringed hand, a shiny brown shoe, vague red clouds of hair. He turned his head slightly and saw the words on her paper all blurred and starting to run. She must have known what to expect, yet she had come unarmed with handkerchief or tissue. Women's tears usually irritated him, but these which rolled down steadily and motivelessly set up an answering pricking in his own eyes. Janet nudged him and thrust a couple of tissues into his hand. He placed them on the brown velvet knee.

'You know who that was?' Janet whispered in the playground as parents and children massed and blocked the narrow iron gate.

'Duncan Rossi's ex-wife, remember she bought the Mill House last year? You know, the racing driver!'

The divorcée passed them, pale and with pink-rimmed eyes, holding by the hand a red-haired boy. Then Gary and Mark hurled themselves on them and had to be zipped into anoraks and the family went home to the house beside the general store and sub-post office which Richard had inherited from his father.

There was the usual nine-fifteen rush in the shop the next morning, of mothers who had delivered their children to school. Mrs Rossi drifted in on the tail-end, in a fur coat and muddy jeans, her dog, tied to the hook outside, howled loudly and tried to spring through the door every time a customer entered or left the shop. She asked Richard to cash a cheque and ordered a lot of groceries to be delivered to the Mill House. She gave no sign of recognition and Richard said nothing.

The sale of the Mill House had been negotiated the previous January, just before her divorce. The car had squelched up the path through the little wood. Duncan at the wheel with a hangover, herself sulking beside him and James in the back with a cold. She had looked at the grey house, the stone heron overlooking the millpond full of yellow leaves, hanks of dun grass, thin blackening nettles, rasping teazels, tangled English melancholy, and thought, 'This will do very well.'

Since then she and the boy had been abroad and it was just a few days since they had taken up residence there, and been surprised by the reddening leaves of the sumach trees in front of the house. All else that remained of cultivation were the Michaelmas daisies and papery disks of honesty. Half a mile up the river that fed their sluggish pond, among brambles' barbed arches and hollow hemlock stems and dried seed heads rattling in the wind, stood a hexagonal concrete pillbox, relic of the war, of which there were many on the North Downs. James had discovered it and intended to occupy it, taking with him matches and food. The entrance turned at a tangent into blackness. The smell drove him back. For a few minutes he stood outside, despising himself, then suddenly turned and fled home, as if a dead Nazi soldier had risen with a rusty bullet hole in his rotted uniform and was pursuing him stiffly and bloodlessly through the wood.

The scarlet sumachs were blazing like sunset at the top of the path. Richard had left the new Cortina Estate at the foot to save the tyres from the sharp stones embedded in deep leaf-falls, and was carrying a heavy carton of groceries. As he walked two bottles clinked together and the gold and colourless liquid slopped in their necks. He thought he heard voices ahead of him and an animal tearing through the undergrowth; Mrs Rossi's bloodhound bitch who left a lemon tang in the misty air. As he followed the citronella trail of antimate through the little wood he heard Mrs Rossi's voice clearly,

'Yes, darling, they are beautiful, but poisonous.' As he passed through their gate he saw a rope of red and green bryony berries looped over the hedge. The boy had disappeared when Richard arrived at the back door.

'Oh it's you, Mr Garlick, stalking us through the woods. I was quite sure it was a murderer. It's so quiet here in the afternoons.'

'I don't think you'll find many murderers in these parts, Mrs Rossi,' he said, putting down the carton on the kitchen table. There were a couple of chairs, several tea chests.

'Settling in now, are you?'

'Not really,' she said, and made no mention of payment, and Richard, wispy-haired with glasses, known in secret moments to his wife as Bunny, didn't like to.

'Thank you very much Mr Garlick.'

'Right then, I'll be off.'

'By the way, I should thank you for the tissues yesterday. It was nice of you.'

'It was nothing.'

Neither seemed capable of dislodging him. At last the bloodhound came to their rescue, rushing in and propelling him with huge fore-paws through the open door.

'Richard! That's the third time Gary's asked you to help him with his model!'

'What? Oh. Right, son, let's be having you!' He rubbed his hands together in simulated eagerness and advanced towards the little pieces of grey plastic.

Because he was in the shop most of the day, Richard was in the position, if he so wanted, of sociologist or chronicler of local mores. He had noticed, over the last year or so, that the topic of property values and house prices, the plight of young couples, discussed in unctuous tones by those who had achieved their mortgage, had given way to the subject of extensions. Janet, behind the little post office grille, among the stamps and leaflets, had been fired by all the talk, and now nothing would do but the loft must be converted into a den for the boys. Richard was sent up a ladder to clear it of junk in readiness for the men who were coming to give an estimate of cost. What Janet termed 'junk' were the dear furnishings of his boyhood, among them glass jars powdered with sherbet crystals and sweet splinters, a cabinet of glass-fronted doors, and a long, bevelled mirror with dark green glass corners and Fry's Cocoa in chocolate coloured letters across its face.

They were eased downstairs and placed, with a pang, outside the shop to await the dustmen. Richard saw his father's watery eye glinting in the mirror and longed for the evidence of his betrayal to be gone. He had hardly spoken to Janet during breakfast.

The dust-cart's dusty buzz was growing louder. Richard sat at the check-out and watched rain accessorise after the fact by blurring the glass and spotting the wood. The shop door crashed open and Mrs Rossi stood there, soaked, bareheaded, accusing.

'You're not consigning those beautiful things to the dustmen!' she stated. 'How much do you want for them?'

'You can have them,' he said surprised.

'Don't be silly. Any antique dealer would snap them up.'

Janet, who had emerged from behind her bars, was beaten back by a rush for Family Allowances and could manage only a twisting scornful finger at her temple over her customers' heads.

'They're yours if you take them away.'

'Right,' she said, 'I will.'

She went out into the rain and attempted to lift a corner of the cabinet but was forced to straighten up, red-faced and defeated. She pulled the mirror away from the wall it leant on and was almost knocked backwards by its weight.

'I'll hire a van,' she said.

The dust-cart was drawing up.

'I'll bring them up this afternoon,' he heard himself say. 'I can borrow a van.'

His reward was the first real smile he had had from her. They went inside.

'Can I talk to you?' she suddenly said quickly. 'I've no friends here. I sensed, I hope I'm right, that you are not badly disposed towards me.'

The shop door jarred, a woman came in, took a wire basket, and after making some decisions, was caught agonisingly between the choice of tomato or fruity sauce. Mrs Rossi hovered at the cheese display.

'Let me persuade you,' said Richard at last, rising and

plucking a bottle of ketchup from the shelf and depositing it in the woman's basket, her mouth opened at his unwonted masterfulness.

'I'll have the other,' she said, replacing his bottle. Two more people came in while she was at the check-out.

'I'll see you later,' said Mrs Rossi, giving up hope and leaving. The bell clanged behind her.

'That's him,' said Mrs Rossi. They were in the sitting room, where the Fry's Cocoa mirror had been propped against the wall. It was carpeted with a green carpet but otherwise was not much more settled than the kitchen, where the glass cabinet and glass sweet jars had been put, and James could be heard clashing a long spoon about in the jars scraping up the sweet sediment. She held out a framed photograph to Richard, of a black curly-haired man in oily overalls, grinning in a crooked laurel-wreath. Richard recognised the face from newspaper and television.

'He's always been a heavy drinker, but he could always get in shape in time for a big race. Lately he's been getting worse and worse. You know he hasn't won anything since the American Grand Prix. He has terrible rages. He's an ice-cream Italian Scot,' she added by way of explanation.

'If ever I told James off, he'd say "Mummy doesn't love you, only Daddy does". Can you imagine? Now I keep having the feeling that he's somewhere around. That he's watching us. He wanted James at the time you know. He's often threatened to kill me.'

She was walking round the room, ran her finger along the windowsill, seemed defeated by dust, and sat down.

'I'm not dependent on him for money,' she said, 'I've got some of my own.'

Richard tried to keep his mind on her problem while watching her mouth move and wondering how it would feel to kiss it.

'Perhaps if you were to take a job?' he ventured. 'Something part-time, so you wouldn't have so much time to brood.'

'Are you offering me a job?' she laughed. 'In the shop? Would you give me a pale blue nylon overall?'

'My wife doesn't object to wearing one.' Even to him it sounded childish and huffy.

She didn't answer.

The dog started to scratch violently. They sat listening to the whirring of claws on skin. At last, when it seemed the air between them must crack, a clock took breath and struck four and released him. He stood up.

'I'd better get back. I shouldn't worry about your ex-husband. He couldn't possibly be here. If you're worried about anything, call the police.' He started for the door with the difficulty he always had when disengaging himself from her presence.

'The phone's not fixed yet,' she said.

'I'll look in tomorrow if you like.'

'Thank you very much,' she said humbly, and walked through the house with him, and the garden, to the front gate, and down to the river bank above the millpond.

'I remember a few years ago we had a particularly wet winter and this pond flooded and – '

He realised she wasn't listening and turned to see her staring at the river with horror on her face.

'What is it? What's the matter?'

She pointed at a whisky bottle in the brown oily water.

'It's his brand,' she whispered.

The bottle did indeed look a sinister emissary bobbing in the water, sucked under the massed leaves in the pond. Light had gone from the sky.

'Nonsense,' Richard told her firmly, 'nonsense, it could have floated down from anywhere.' He realised she was clutching his arm.

'Go in now, it's getting cold. I'll look in tomorrow. Why don't you get someone, a friend, to come and stay?'

'I have.'

As he left her Richard had the distinct feeling that Mrs Rossi was slightly crazy, deranged; perhaps by her divorce.

'You haven't forgotten that it's the stoolball AGM have you?' said Janet. 'I'll be back by about ten, I expect.'

Richard had supervised the boys' bath and they were playing in the bedroom. He went up to tell them to go to bed. Mark was fooling about with a pair of plastic binoculars.

'Let's have a look,' said Richard. He hung them round his neck and went to the window.

'These could be very useful,' he said. 'For observing wildlife or spying on the neighbours.' He put them to his eyes and adjusted the focus. They were surprisingly powerful and picked out the lighted panes of the village hall windows, stars and clouds in the black sky, the church spire against the moon. He raked them through the woods, up to the Mill House. Light shone in the sitting room and two upstairs windows. He looked beyond the house up river. From the black mass of the river bank rose a thin twist of grey smoke. Realisation kicked him in the stomach. Someone was in the pillbox, watching the Mill House, waiting. Rossi.

'Come on, Daddy, let's have a go!' Richard handed back the glasses, feeling sick and sat on the bed. His immediate impulse was to rush out, up to the Mill House. Janet was out, he would have to wait until the boys were asleep. He hustled them into bed and kissed each tenderly, with the fear that he might not see them again, and went downstairs, put on coat and gloves, and waited. The thought came to him that it would be wiser to call the police, but he dismissed it. He had never in his life been called on to do anything even slightly frightening or dangerous; he was an eater of meals on time, a sleeper in soft beds, wearer of slippers. His only brush with fear was when Janet went into hospital to have the boys. He crept upstairs and removed the book from Gary's sleeping hand and straightened the Action Man on Mark's pillow. He checked the central heating and closed the front door quietly behind him.

He walked quickly through the village, meeting no one,

and ran across the wet field and into the wood. Sharp stones pierced the soles of his shoes as he ran. Pain in his lungs bent him double on the front doorstep as he lifted a finger to the bell. It drilled through the house, then silence blotted its soundwaves. He rang again and again, desperately. Then realising why she wouldn't answer, sensing her terror in the locked house, poked open the letter box to call through it. Iron choked his voice, his head swelled like a black balloon. He tried to claw the fingers from his throat, then swung his foot back and kicked hard where he sensed his attacker's legs were. It struck home, and Richard fell back against the door as the fingers fell away. Rossi was rolling on the ground, a knife beside him. Richard grabbed it and threw it in a weak shoulder-wrenching underarm. A splash sounded. Rossi was rising. Richard pulled back his fist, shutting his eyes, and cracked it on to his jaw, and again. Pain jarred up his arm. He took off his glove to suck his knuckle, and realised that Rossi had been overcome not just by his blows but by the alcohol whose fumes were being pumped in reeking gusts from his panting body. He pulled himself up and stumbled through the front garden. Richard sat on the step, wiping his glasses which he hadn't thought to remove. Rossi belched as he disappeared. This crude eructation hanging in the night sky filled Richard with rage against him and his terrorising of Rose. He set off after him. His footsteps spurred Rossi into a lurching run. He turned not right, into the wood, but left along the lane that led to the sand quarry. For a moment Richard saw him spreadeagled against the high wire fence like an escaping prisoner, then he was over. Richard found the gate and climbed to the top, jumped and fell into soft sand. A ghostly convoy of bulldozers stood. Rossi was running across the flat towards pale mountains of sand. A high wooden building on stilts bulked against the sky. The word 'corrosive' glittered in the moonlight on a rusty tank. Richard lost Rossi in the white sandscape, his shoes were full and heavy, he stopped running and stood, air swirling round him like black ectoplasm, his heart banging, yet he was not afraid.

Suddenly he knew that it was Rossi's fear, not his own that he felt, and that Rossi was very near. He knew his enemy and Rossi did not. For all he knew Richard might be a fiend from hell. Rossi stumbled round the base of a sandhill. Richard started after him, his joints moved slickly, blood oiling his muscles. He was gaining on Rossi and could hear sawing breaths in his chest. Rossi took a despairing look over his shoulder and made for a giant crane or dinosaur whose neck stretched out some thirty feet over the highest mountain. Thick raindrops were pitting the sand. Richard reached the crane and saw Rossi climb over the cab and on to the monster's neck. The rungs must have been greasy with rain, but Rossi climbed on towards the top, where he must surely be trapped, and crawled dark and terrified against the sky.

Richard was suddenly sick of it all.

'I'm going home!' he shouted. 'Come down.'

The only words used between them. He turned to go, as if ground was falling away from his own tingling feet, arms tearing from their sockets, chest caving with the altitude.

As, ground spinning under him, he turned to see if Rossi was descending, he saw him hanging, kicking wildly from the crane, kicking, struggling to hook his legs back up. His legs went still, he dangled, his fingers slowly opened out and he plummeted silently into the heart of the soft volcano. Rivers of sand ran down the sides, trickled, and stopped.

Richard stood in the rain. He looked round at the sandscape undisturbed under the moon, the still machinery. There was nothing to be done. To reach Rossi he too must leap from the crane and suffocate in sand. Help would be too late.

He turned and ran.

While the bath was running he stood in the clouds of steam shaking every grain of sand from his sock and shoes, and all his clothes into the basin. Rain without and steam within; he lay back in the water and watched the black window pane liquify. The rims of his nails were greenish with packed sand. He took the nailbrush.

Janet's key twisted in the lock; he attempted a snatch of the St Matthew Passion, but his throat choked up as if with sand.

'We've been asked to a party tomorrow,' came Janet's voice.

Luckily, it was Wednesday. Rose Rossi didn't come in in the morning and the shop closed in the afternoon. Alone in the house, golden rod beckoning like false blonde women at the window, Richard saw how trees soughed and leaves fell, the church clock struck and cars passed, the world went on and the loss of one of its sons in a sandhill seemed to matter not at all. So this is all we are worth, he thought. None of us matters at all.

Married couples were jogging round the through-lounge of the party givers' house. The host claimed Janet, and Richard moved towards the lush buffet. He became aware of a strange noise below the music, a sort of drone. He looked round and saw that all the couples were singing the words of the songs of their youth, slightly behind the record, and Janet, eyes closed, was murmuring them too, and he only wanted to be with Rose Rossi. He went through to the kitchen.

'Do you remember,' a woman was saying, 'how, at parties when we were young, someone was always sick, and someone lost a shoe?'

'And when they put the lights out, all the girls had to sit on a boy's knee and "snog", whether they wanted to or not?' said another.

'Just getting a breath of fresh air,' said Richard as he passed unnoticed through the back door.

He drove up to the Mill House, not caring any longer about his tyres, and was shocked by a strange car parked outside the gate. He was furious; he kicked its tyre. Her friend must have come. He walked round the house, wondering what excuse he could give for arriving. Outside the sitting room window he stopped.

There, caught in the Fry's Cocoa mirror were Rose and

her friend. The friend's hair was pulled back in Rose Rossi's grasp as she kissed her mouth.

He wandered round the woods, sent stones crashing into the millpond and disturbed no one. Eventually, frozen, he drove back to the party. The smell of black coffee hit him as he walked in. Janet was in the kitchen seated on a stool with her head in her chest. He shook her shoulder, she looked up at him sideways and mumbled,

'I've lost my shoe.'

The Stained-Glass Door

Jean MacAllister's rather large white face, which had hung soft and dreamy in the steam of her drinking chocolate, hardened as she turned from the kitchen window.

'She's out there again.'

Nigel MacAllister yawned; scratching his chest, catching his finger in a grey curl.

'She's probably lonely. Bored. Anyway she'll be gone soon. You know how those people come and go. . . .'

'She doesn't. She's going in now, grinding out a cigarette with her foot. That lawn must be knee-deep in cigarette butts.'

'If you can call it a lawn any more.'

'It was such a lovely garden. You'd think the Council. . . .'

Nigel yawned again; he had heard it all before – that beautiful house, the mirror image of their own, taken over by the Council; the blanket looped across the window instead of curtains, the rusting cars, the broken glass, the language. He gave his wife a slap, almost too hard, as she hung the washed mugs on their hooks.

'Come on then, or we won't get up in the morning.'

They went upstairs.

'Nigel – is anything wrong?'

'I told you, I've got problems at work.'

'Actually, you didn't.'

As the sound of a plane ebbed in the darkness a rumbling came from Nigel's side of the bed and Jean's stomach gave a timid answering bleat. She could have felt sorry for those two stomachs had they lain side by side in white bloody trays in a butcher's window, which was how, for a moment, she saw them.

The following evening when Jean arrived home from her upholstery class with her little hammer, bristling with tacks, although nothing in that house needed re-upholstering – there were no children or animals to kick and claw, not even any visiting nieces and nephews – she stood for a moment looking at the sky. A jewelled insect was homing in on Gatwick through the stars. The house next door was in darkness, but the girl in the downstairs flat had neglected to pull down the blanket across the window and Jean saw her, in the light of a streetlamp, asleep on a divan, hair spread out, thumb in mouth.

As on almost every morning, Jean stood at the head of the stairs, restored and reassured by her house; the morning sunshine filtering through the stained-glass door, throwing pale pink and green and yellow bars and diamonds and lozenges of light onto the carpet, gilding the hall table, the flowers in the iridescent glass; the empty rooms unfolding quietly from the hall. Several brown envelopes lay on the mat; they were all that seemed to come nowadays. She hardly glanced at them as she threw them onto the sideboard.

Boring bills. She left all that side of things to Nigel.

Later, although it was not yet ten o'clock, in her cotton dress and sandals, she was beaded with sweat by the time she reached the High Street. Outside the baker's she bumped into a woman and looked into her powdered face, a red slick of lipstick or jam in icing sugar, and realised that this oozing doughnut had been driven, at this early hour, to pound the hot pavements to the off-licence; tell-tale bottles clashed glassily in her bag. Jean turned with relief to the wholesome shiny sticks of bread.

Later again that morning she saw, through a fine pink mist of Windowlene, the girl from next door with her baby on her hip, a plastic bag of washing on the seat of the pushchair, setting off for the launderette. Really, there would seem nothing to connect those two, the skinny blonde girl and the unarguably coffee-coloured baby; except that the tiny brown hand was tangled in the lank hair like a baby animal's clinging onto its mother's fur. As she rubbed the window clear it blurred unaccountably.

With a heavy hand she sliced slabs of French bread for the bread and cheese lunch she was holding, the proceeds from which were to go to Oxfam. Her friends pecked like starlings with greasy beaks; her bread hovered in the air as first Nigel, then the girl next door, superimposed themselves on the chatter about children's 'O' level options, a topic of very limited interest to Jean.

She sighed and smeared her bread with butter and pickle.

'I'm starving,' she remarked through a mouthful of

159

piercing crust. 'Let's take our coffee onto the patio,' she suggested, but the sunny stones were splintered by pop music from a radio next door.

'Will you turn that bloody thing down!' She suddenly erupted in a brown geyser of hot coffee. Her friends mopped and soothed, but all at once realised how time had flown and that so must they.

The MacAllisters had brought their friends, Peter and Mary, back to supper after a concert at the Fairfield Halls. Blue skeins of cigar smoke wound over the coffee cups, binding them, still softened by music and golden-bellied wood, together. The doorbell burst blue ropes, shattered golden wood. Jean returned from answering it.

'It was that girl from next door. Mandy. She wanted to use the telephone. I told her to use the callbox on the corner.' Her voice rose.

'It was for her own good. These people have got to stand on their own two feet. That's the trouble with the Welfare State, it makes people lazy. Apathetic. Soft. I mean, Nigel's worked damned hard for everything we've got!'

She stalked into the kitchen, clashing bowls, leaving Nigel and Mary to rekindle a cigar and prod a candle with a dead match, dropping ugly black specks into the rosy wax. Peter followed with a couple of spoons.

'I wish she'd go!' Jean burst out. 'I'm sick of her. Always looming. Intruding. Imposing her miserable life on mine. I mean . . .' above the thunderous tap, wrenching pink rubber gloves onto her fingers, 'it's not my fault. . . .'

Peter sidestepped the spray as the water hit a fork and turned off the tap.

'Of course it's not your fault. Your trouble is, you care too much about other people. You're too sensitive.'

The next morning Mary telephoned. 'Have you been in the copse lately?'

'No. Why?'

'There are masses of blackberries there. Beauties. Come and have a bite of lunch after yoga and we'll go black-berrying.'

'If you like.'

The receiver gave a squawk, almost a hurt sound, as she put it down on her friend's voice.

She had not intended to bulge in her leotard and black tights that morning, her head achy with too much wine the night before, and Mary's wholemeal pizza would undo any benefit the exercise might give; but the half-empty freezer groaned like a threatening ice-floe for the soft fruit and she had made no jam yet. The afternoon found them in the copse armed with Tupperware containers. Jean felt the knots that Yoga had failed to untie dissolve in the sun and bird song as she gazed at a branch that bore bud, white flower, hard green berry, solid jelly brushed with red and the rich black culmination; on a single stem. Mary grabbed her arm.

'What's that noise?'

A blackbird shrieked. Over their banging hearts a steady shuffling sound came nearer. The middle-aged women clutched each other among spilled berries. It came towards them.

A baby broke through the undergrowth. It crawled; laughing through lips juicy with squashed blackberries. Mandy strode up and scooped the baby, who kicked its legs in delight, under her arm and was gone, but not before they had seen her face, streaked with tears and dirt where an earthy hand had brushed them away.

Although they continued to pick greedily, the gloss was gone from the afternoon. As Jean hurried past the house next door, through the smell of a blocked drain, it seemed to lunge at her; her own house in a distorting mirror.

It seemed that she had lost the art of making jam. She boiled and boiled; the house was filled with the smell of apples and blackberries but the jam would not set.

Hot uneasy nights when she and Nigel sweated separately in bed followed hot days when Jean could do nothing but lie on the grass. The sprinkler on the lawn brought a cool damp hour on some evenings, then she did the ironing, alone in the house; through a glaze of gin. She ceased to notice the light falling through the stained-glass door; the stems of the flowers on the hall table swelled and stank; the pile of unopened brown envelopes on the dusty sideboard grew higher.

She woke one night, whimpering; her silky nightdress clinging like a rag. Unhappy noises came from the hot cages next door. Someone was shouting, the baby was crying, glass smashed.

'Nigel,' she whispered in the darkness of her life grown rotten, 'Nigel.'

With a groan, he fell on her; she felt a tear fall onto her neck and burn the hollow of her collarbone.

Tomorrow she would clean the house, cook a wonderful meal, and over it get Nigel to tell her what was wrong. Together they would tackle and beat the foe, whatever it was. She nestled against the dear body that had been given into her care and moaned softly to think that he had not been able to trust himself to her.

It was afternoon by the time she was able to get onto the patio with the *Telegraph* crossword. In the gleaming house were flowers and such beautiful still lifes of fruit and vegetables that she would be reluctant to put them to the knife. She twirled the pen in her fingers; the sun struck its transparent plastic facets, threw revolving rainbows on the newsprint. Something dropped to the grass. A pear had fallen from the tree in next door's garden. The tree was heavy with golden fruit against the blue; ripe, heavy, going to waste. A bird even had its beak in one. She looked at the house. The family upstairs was out. The drug addicts in the middle flat were either asleep or dead. Mandy's radio was silent.

She was on the wall almost before she knew it. The pears fell into her hands and spread skirt. Scented flesh broke against her teeth. Suddenly, in a cracking of branches, Mandy's face thrust through the leaves. Jean jumped, breaking twigs, grazing the backs of her thighs on the wall and landed heavily on all fours. She looked up over her shoulder, like a dog. Mandy was standing on the wall, gigantic against the sky, hurling pears at her, shouting,

'You want it all, don't you? You want the lot! Well, go on then, take it! Have the bloody pears!'

163

Jean caught a pear as she fled inside. It lay in her hand, gilded, wormy.

By six o'clock the shameful incident, marinated all afternoon in her mind, was sufficiently tenderised and trimmed to be offered as an amusing anecdote to Nigel when he came home. But he did not come home.

Jean woke on the sofa to a smell of burning from the oven and to find that someone had drunk all the wine. She lifted the receiver to ring the police and let it fall. She knew that he had left her. Days and nights passed. Someone. There must be someone. Not her friends. There was only Mandy. Fellow sufferer. Betrayed. But golden pears blocked her path. Jean seized two withered apples from the fruit bowl, smiling in anticipation of Mandy's face as she understood the peace offering. There was a light behind the blanket, and music. Jean pressed and pressed the broken bell.

'There'll be a heartache tonight, heartache tonight . . .' came thumping through the cracked stained glass.

Later she realised that she had been sitting for a long time in the skeleton of a chair. She had forgotten all about her upholstery class. She went to the telephone.

'Peter. How are you? It's Jean. Is Mary there?'

'Jean! Are you all right?'

'Of course, I'm all right. I merely wanted to ask Mary if she had any of that red Dralon left. Why shouldn't I be all right?'

'It's just that it's three o'clock in the morning. . . .'

Jean was woken by an unfamiliar noise from next door. Laughter. Feet were going up and down the path. She threw back the duvet and ran to the window.

Mandy was leaving in a taxi.

Jean struggled with the window and forced it open. She wanted to say something, make everything all right. She clawed through the wardrobe and pulled out a bag. 'Mandy!' The car backfired a contemptuous burst of grey smoke at her. Mandy was gone. Escaped. Victorious. Jean hurled the bag through the window. It burst, spilling spurned, never-needed baby clothes over the road.

Mary might have telephoned her, but she would not have got through, because that morning the phone was cut off.

The man in the Social Security office gave Jean a funny look as she sat down in the peeling grey and yellow room. She knew she looked all right; she had checked in the 'ladies' in the pub.

'How was Brittany?' she asked brightly. He stared. 'Don't you remember? I came in year or so ago about my holiday insurance and we discovered that we were going to the same place.' Evidently he did not remember.

The weather became colder. Jean lay shivering in the aftermath of a dream in which she and Nigel were putting up the tent on a camp-site and Nigel had started to hammer the tent-peg into her head. She realised that it was more than a year since he had gone. She could still hear the hammering. A man was fixing a 'For sale' sign to the fence. She remembered the face of a woman outside the baker's, whom she had despised as a doughnut. Now it was she who lay on the edge of a bed grown too vast; a white soggy meringue left on the side of someone's plate.

Surely she had had most need of blessing? Jean came down the church aisle more unsteadily than was possible from the mouthful of wine, although she had not risen from the altar rail after receiving the Sacrament. She had stretched out her hands again for the cup, but the blue glassy eyes of the vicar had cut them and passed over her.

If afterwards, in the porch, his white sleeve billowed for a moment like the sail of a rescue ship, it was at once drowned by a wave of eager young faces. A woman's voice called her name tentatively as she stumbled over the humpbacked gravestones, grey whales and basking sharks with granite teeth, that reared under her feet. She cursed herself for putting those two pound notes in the collection. Much good it had done her. Her heart was already thumping with the beginnings of shame. There was only one way, impossible now, to soothe it. Let soft seas of alcohol lap over the brain. She walked into the terrible yawning dry jaws of afternoon.

Something made her stop and look in her purse. She pulled out two pound notes. The miraculous green paper shook in her fingers. She must have put a pawn ticket in the collection bag.

'Thank you, God,' she said as she went into the off-licence.

Tired, and buffeted by Christmas shoppers, Jean was thankful to get home. How pretty the holly wreath looked, festive against the stained glass. Nigel must have done it to surprise her. She knelt to kiss its berries; the cold prickles grazed her face. Her key wouldn't fit. She rattled and rattled. Tears burst from her eyes as she put her mouth to the letterbox, smearing the polished brass.

'Nigel,' she called. 'Nigel! I can't open the door!'

He opened it in a rush of spicy air. But it wasn't Nigel. A boy stood staring at her.

'Mum,' he shouted, 'Mu-um!'

She scrambled up. The holly had scratched her lip. With the metallic taste of blood she remembered. She turned back up the slushy path and into the house next door.

She kicked off her shoes and lit the fire and sat down to see what she had bought. A Bird's Trifle. How odd. Still, there was a little milk; it wouldn't matter if it had gone off slightly. Her coat fell open and she confronted a thigh; she must have forgotten to put her skirt on. She sat in her leotard stroking in pity the poor white flesh marbled with cold. The light went out. The gas fire went out.

In the light, from the streetlamp, falling through the blanket looped across the window she turned to the trifle. The Dream Topping. The hundreds and thousands melting in rainbow drizzle.

167

Babies in Rhinestones

The Alfred Ellis School of Fine Art and the Araidne Elliot School of Dance and Drama stood semi-detached from one another behind a small tearful shrubbery of mahonia and hypericum, snowberries, bitter blue currants, spotted laurel and pink watery globes of berberis spiked on their own thorns. A crooked hedge of yellow-berried holly divided the two gardens. The artist's was distinguished by a rusting iron sculpture, while Miss Elliot's, or Madame as she was addressed by her pupils, held a grey polystyrene cupidon bearing a shell of muddy water.

In the green gloom of his hall Alfred Ellis held up a letter to the light to see if it contained any money. It was in fact addressed to Araidne Elliot and had come through the wrong door. As he crumpled it into his pocket he wondered again if she knew that her name should be Ariadne. He fancied, as he passed the half open door of his front room, or atelier, that something moved, but when he went in all the easels were posing woodenly in their places. In the kitchen he poured boiling water onto an old teabag and was sitting down to read the paper when a round striped ginger face appeared at the window.

'Good morning, Ginger,' he said as he let in the cat.

'I suppose you want your breakfast. I was about to read the Deaths, to see if I had died recently. Now I shall never know.' He brushed at the bouquets of smudgy paw marks on the black words and poured out a bowl of milk.

Dead or alive, half an hour later he set off for the shops. Ginger ran down the path before him. At the same time his neighbour emerged from her gate, struggling with a green umbrella. Araidne Elliot seemed more at the mercy of the elements than other people; the mild late autumn rain had, on her walk down the garden path, reduced her piled-up hair to a spangled ruin sliding from its combs. A scarlet mahonia leaf was slicked to the toe of her boot. A cluster of red glass berries dangled from each ear.

'Miss Elliot, you look the very spirit of autumn. . . .'

She did not reply, being unsure, as so often, if he was being unpleasant, and looked down at Ginger who was rolling on his back on the pavement at their feet, displaying his belly where the stripes dissolved into a pool of milky fur.

'Home, Rufus!' she said sharply. 'You can't come to the library with me.'

'Rufus?'

She blushed. 'I call him that. I don't know his real name – he's not really mine, I'm afraid. He just walked in one day and made himself at home. He always comes for his breakfast and sometimes he stays the night. He sleeps on my bed.' She blushed again. 'I wish I could keep him, but he's obviously got a home. . . .'

'His breakfast?' repeated Alfred Ellis. 'That's impossible!'

170

'Oh yes, every day, but the funny thing is, he won't touch milk!'

'You little tart, Ginger,' he said softly, inserting a not very gentle toe into the cat's wanton chest. Ginger gathered up his legs and departed, tail worn low, between two branches of a spiraea.

'What a very unpleasant shrub that is,' said Alfred Ellis.

'How can you say that,' she cried. 'All flowers are lovely.'

Her doubts about him as an artist tumbled through her head; a rat's skull on the windowsill, a drain blocked with dead leaves, his profile like a battered boxer's, the sculpture like a rusting vegetable rack in his garden. They walked on.

'This is yours, I think.' 'He fished in the pocket of his stained corduroy trousers and handed her the letter.

'Not bad news, I trust?' he capered at her side, squinting over her shoulder.

'Not at all. Just a bill,' she said coldly, putting it in her bag.

'Manage to spell your name right, did they?'

'I don't know, I didn't look. Why?'

He could hardly tell her that every time he saw the board outside her house he had to suppress an urge to seize a paintbrush and alter it.

'Those grey trousers with bald knees make him look like an old elephant who has been in the zoo too long,' she was thinking as they crossed the railway tracks at the level crossing. Alfred Ellis suddenly stopped and waved an arm at a large bronze ballerina pirouetting in the wind.

'Ah, Dame Margot!' he cried. 'An inspiration to us all,

171

eh Miss Elliot? Born plain Alice Marks in this very borough and still dancing away in all weathers. . . .'

She strode away, her feet almost at right angles, a dancer in dudgeon. He laughed. He was often bored and it amused him to provoke his neighbour. He was often lonely too, and was disproportionately hurt by the news that his friend Ginger was so free with his favours.

He crossed the road and forced to return his greeting an ex-pupil who was obviously about to cut him.

'I thought of you on Saturday,' she admitted. 'Yes, I was helping with the school Autumn Fayre and one of your pictures turned up on the bric-à-brac stall. I almost bought it, but the frame was in such poor condition. . . .'

The artist turned away with what might have been a laugh.

He thought about her as he walked; one of too many ladies striding about the town with shopping trolleys, whose skin from years of smiling at the antics of dogs and children and husbands creased into fans of angst at the eyes, whose arms were muscled from turning over the pages of *Which* and cookery books borrowed from the library; they never had time to read fiction; whose faces were still faintly tanned from their camping holiday in France where they had sat in the passenger seat of the car with maps and Blue Guides and Red Guides on their laps, reflecting that if they had gone to Cornwall they would not be boiling along between endless fields of sweetcorn and poplars; who had once suggested that they might stop and look at a cathedral, but had been hooted down by the rest of the family – and anyway the 'O' Level results hung in a thundercloud on the horizon; who sometimes came to his art classes to draw dead grasses and bunches of dried honesty.

He was struck by a house garlanded with a green climbing plant and stood watching the wind lifting the leaves so that the house looked airy and insubstantial, as if it might take wing, and remembered a birthday cake that his grandmother had sent him when he was a boy, white icing and green maidenhair fern, and marvelled that someone should once have thought him worth such a cake. A twist of smoke from his thin cigarette burned his eye. The pure white icing attacked his stained teeth as he went into the greengrocer's to buy the still life for his morning class. He was crossing the car park on his way home when he passed a stall selling fresh fish, cockles and mussels. He retraced his steps. So, banging his shin on the metal rim of a bucket of briny shells, he began his campaign of seduction.

'Oysters,' he said, his teeth glistening in his beard.

'We haven't any.'

He looked over white fluted shells holding tremulous raw eggs.

'Give me a mackerel. The bluest you have.'

In his mind's eye he saw the mackerel with a lemon on a plate.

He was painting it that afternoon, the blue fish curved on the white oval plate, the lemon with the faintest blush of green, beside the darkening window when he saw a figure slinking through the black grass under the holly hedge. He flung open the window and, wrecking his still life, waved the fish at the cat. Ginger stopped, sniffed, laid back his ears, lifted a loyal paw in the direction of Araidne's house, then leaped through the window.

'Gotcha!' Alfred slammed it shut. Soon heavy swirls of fishy steam mingled with the smell of linseed oil and paint and Ginger was arching his back, walking up and down the kitchen table, purring in anticipation. Half an hour later he lay replete and Alfred Ellis smirked and wiped his greasy fingers on his trousers as the sound of 'Puss, Puss, Puss' came through the rain. Ginger raised an ear, shook his head and stuck out a hind leg to wash. A cloudy eye watched from the draining board.

In the morning Araidne Elliot had to plug in the electric fire to take the chill off the air before the Tinies' Tap Class.

'Bit chilly in here, isn't it?' said a mother, pulling her fur coat around herself.

'We'll soon warm up,' replied Araidne listlessly. Rufus. She supposed he was the only person who loved her.

'Yes, well. Tara's only just got over a shocking cough. I was in two minds whether to bring her. She was barking all night.'

Araidne's ears, on either side of her hairnet, strained to hear a miaow. She looked in despair at her class. The cold was marbling the Tinies' thighs pink and blue to match their leotards and headbands. They seemed to troop incessantly to the toilet, returning with their leotards hiked up over their knickers. She feared that most of them had not washed their hands.

'I'm putting on my top hat. . . .'

If she was to fit a lock on the bathroom door, she thought as she danced, that took two-pence pieces . . . her cane flashed dangerously.

'. . . polishing my nails.'

In a dusty corner lay an unperformed revue: 'Babies in Rhinestones,' written and choreographed by Araidne Elliot, in which strings of sparkling babes, shimmering in precision, crisscrossed a vast stage under a spinning prismatic globe, scattered like broken jewellery, and grouped and regrouped in endless stars, rings, necklaces, bangles, tiaras of rainbow glass.

On the other side of the wall Alfred Ellis elicited some disapproval from his students as he executed a bit of inelegant hoofing through the easels to the tap, tap, tap of forty little shoes and one clacking big pair.

'Really, Mr Ellis, that music is most distracting!'

'Lovely chiaroscuro on that teasel, Mrs Wyndham Lewis,' he attempted to placate her, 'If I might suggest . . . the onions. . . .'

He added a few strokes of charcoal.

'I think I preferred it as it was,' she said, recoiling from his fishy breath.

'What I object to,' murmured one to another, 'is the fact that one can never finish anything. One embarks on a *nature morte* one lesson, only to find that he's eaten it by the next . . . most unprofessional.'

Araidne could hardly close the front door quickly enough; it clipped the heels of the last mummy, and forced herself to wait until the last car had pulled away before rushing out to check the gutters for a furry body.

She wondered if she would be able to pick it up. Her hair escaped like a catch of eels from its net as she stooped.

'Looking for something, Miss Elliot?'

The loathsome artist was grinning over his gate. She strode on, blushing. Rufus could be presumed alive so far, at least. She thought of his white-tipped paws, his meticulously striped tail, its white tip. She told herself that she was being absurd; he had simply been kept indoors; the people he lived, or condescended to lodge, with, showing some sense of responsibility at last. Nevertheless she scanned every garden that she passed and encountered some striped and tabby persons, but not the face of the beloved. She wandered for some time and at just after one o'clock arrived, or found herself, in a little road near the station. The few small shops were shut. There was nobody about; the little terraced houses looked empty. She heard her heels on the pavement and suddenly felt dispossessed, as if she was in a Tennessee Williams's movie. *The Fugitive Kind*. She hesitated in front of a phone box; there was no one to call. It was a relief to arrive in the High Street. She purchased a bottle of pallid rosé and a stiff slice of Camembert to take to the end of term party of her French class, an event to which she looked forward with some gloom. Experience had taught her to avoid the Evening Institute on the first evening of the spring term, when, new aftershave failing to mask the scent of loneliness, people would be required to give details of their sad Christmases in French.

'On m'a donné beaucoup de cadeaux – er – le smoker's

candle, le déodorant, le très petit pudding de Noel de Madame Peek. . . .'

It was as she came out of the delicatessen that she saw, slouching along with a baby buggy, cigarette in hand, her one-time star pupil, the one for whom she had had the highest hopes. Could it be three years ago that she had brought down the house with her rendition of 'Bring on the Clowns'?

'Karen!'

'Madame!' She dropped her cigarette.

'What's his name?' She peered into the buggy.

'Neil.'

'I suppose we'll be seeing Neil in the Tinies' Class soon?' She chucked him awkwardly under the wet chin. 'I could do with a nice boy. . . .'

'Couldn't we all?' replied her ex-pupil.

Araidne's eyes filled with tears. She couldn't resist calling after her in a slightly wavery voice,

'Shoulders back, Karen, and do tuck your tail in!'

While the riches of the sea, sardines painted in silver leaf, shrimps like pink corals, saucy pilchards, fins and tails, poured out in the artist's kitchen and Ginger waxed fat and indolent, his whiskers standing out from his round head in glossy quills, Araidne Elliot grew as boney and twitchy as a hooked hake. Alfred Ellis expected her daily to ask if he had seen the cat, but she did not come.

One morning, while picking a branch of snowberries from the front garden, he saw, further up the road, on the opposite side, a yellow removal van. He went to investigate and saw carried into the van a wicker basket whose lid was pushed open by a ginger face; it flapped shut, and then a striped tail flicked out in farewell.

'Mr Ellis!' Araidne was at her open window with a letter in her hand. 'I'm afraid the postman has muddled our mail again.'

He took it, and seeing the postmark almost ran to his own house, without a word of thanks or a word about Ginger's departure. It was from a man who owned a small gallery in Gravesend, who had seen some of Ellis's paintings in the Salon de Refusés of the South Surrey Arts Society exhibition and proposed to visit him with a view to mounting one-man show of his work. He gobbled gleefully at what would have been Ginger's supper as he read and re-read the letter until it was creased and oily.

That evening he took down a large prepared canvas which had stood empty for months and would now receive his masterwork, the heart of his exhibition, the flowering of his genius; but his brush kept dancing to a faint beat coming through the wall – 'From the top again, please Mrs Taylor' – and the image of Araidne's old accompanist's resigned shoulders at the keyboard superimposed itself on the canvas, so eventually he had to admit defeat and switch on 'Dallas'. Later he went for a walk. It had rained, but now the air was frosty, the ivy all diamanté, the hedges cold and hard like marcasite.

'Rufus . . . Rufus,' came palely through the starlight.

The Muse was still recalcitrant the next morning, so he thought that he might seduce her with a pint or two in convivial company. He saw Araidne in the High Street; she saw him too and turned, but too late; he was performing a grotesque dance at her on the pavement, and whistling.

'I'm sorry if my music disturbed you,' she said stiffly. 'I do have a living to make. . . .'

'Please don't apologise. The clog dance from "La Fille Mal Gardé" just happens to be my very, very, all-time favourite – especially when I'm trying to work.'

'Excuse me.'

He followed her at a distance and entered a shop behind her. She placed her basket on the counter and took out a packet.

'These tights aren't at all what I wanted.'

'What do you want then?'

She burst into tears, grabbed her basket, and ran out of the shop.

Alfred Ellis winked at the astonished assistant, but he could have wept too. Before she had fled he had looked into her basket: a packet of Fishy Treats, two frozen cod steaks and a library book, *Some Tame Gazelle* by Barbara Pym.

In the pub he muttered into his beer, attracting a fishy glance from the landlord who knew him of old. The shop assistant had asked her what she wanted and the book had replied for her: 'Something to love, oh, something to love.'

'Some tame gazelle, or some gentle dove . . . give me a whisky, George. Better make it a double.'

The seduction of Ginger seemed less amusing now.

'Something to love, oh, something to love,' he murmured

to the fruit machine as it turned up two lemons and a raspberry. He put a coin in the jukebox to drown the rusty voice of shame, but he had to go and look for her.

'Miss Elliot, please. Will you come and have a drink with me. Don't run away. I've got something to tell you. It's most important. It's about Rufus.'

He saw her turn as white as the snowberries in his garden, as red as their twigs, and blanch again.

Two hours later two slightly tear-stained dishevelled people with foolish smiles, clutching a cardboard cat-carrier, a wicker basket, a sack of cat litter, a plastic tray and a carrier bag of tins, struggled down the High Street.

'I think Beulah for the little black one, what do you think?' Alfred Ellis was saying.

Araidne caught sight of their reflection in a shop window.

'Goodness, we almost look like a couple,' she thought. She said, 'We want to give them nice names, sensible names, that won't embarrass them when they go to school – grow up, I mean. Names are so important, don't you think?'

'I hated mine when I was a boy. Did you like yours?'

'I chose it.' She admitted. 'My real name's Gwen. I saw the name Araidne in a book and I thought it was so beautiful and romantic. So when I opened the dancing school I changed it to Araidne.'

'Ah,' he said.

'What about Tom for the boy? Can we put these down for a minute? My arms are breaking. Oh, I can hear a little voice! Oh, we'll soon be home, darlings.'

Outside their houses he turned to go into his, she into hers. The cat carrier was almost torn in two. Instant sobriety, hangover, realisation of what they had done. They stood on the pavement staring at one another. A cold wind blew up; the miaows from the box grew wilder.

'Whose dumb idea was this anyway?'

'Yours, I think. But don't worry, I'm taking them.'

'Oh no, you don't!'

'I refuse to stand here brawling in the street. Give me those kittens!'

She tried to snatch them, but he broke free and bolted down his path with them and she grabbed the rest of the stuff and hurried after him lest she be locked out and lose them altogether.

In his kitchen he set the box on the floor and opened it and they knelt on either side gazing at the two tiny faces, one black, one marked like a pansy, looking up, pink and black mouths opening on teeth as sharp as pins. Then, gently, with his big stained fingers, he lifted the kittens out, and on little ricketty-looking legs they entered into their kingdom. Alfred Ellis capitalised on Araidne's softened look by opening a bottle of wine; she opened a tin of evaporated milk.

'Let's go into the other room, where it's more comfortable,' he said, 'and try and think of some solution. Perhaps they should stay here tonight, anyway, as they seem to be making themselves at home. . . .'

Some hours later two empty bottles and a pile of dirty plates stood on the table. Blue cigarette smoke lay flat across the air like branches of a cedar tree. Araidne lay heavy-eyed on the sofa with the kittens asleep in her lap. A gentle purring could be heard.

'Perhaps you should all stay the night,' said Alfred Ellis, putting a balloon of brandy to his lips. 'It would be upsetting for the kittens if you should go now. . . .'

Araidne slunk up her path in the morning, feeling very ill, just in time to pre-empt her morning class.

'From the top, Mrs Taylor. But pianissimo, please.'

She was obviously not in a good mood when she returned.

'Switch that thing off! I've got the most appalling headache in the history of the world. What on earth are you doing?' She shouted, wrenching the plug of his Black and Decker from the socket.

'It's the perfect solution,' he said, his hair white with plaster dust. I'm drilling a passage from my house to yours so that the kittens can come and go as they please. There's half a Disprin left, if you want it,' he added.

As he spoke a crack zig-zagged through the plaster, then another.

'Oh dear. Perhaps we'd better take the whole wall down?'

The man from the gallery at Gravesend rang and rang the doorbell, and at last walked round the side of the house and looked through the window. The hindquarters of a man, covered in plaster and brick dust, were wriggling through a hole in the wall, while a woman, with a savage look on her face, stood in a lumpy sea of broken plaster, with two kittens running about her shoulders and biting her distracted hair, gulping a glass of water and grasping an electric drill as if she might plunge it into her companion's disappearing leg. He was a timid man, and he crept away.

The kittens proved to be bad wild infants who tore up canvasses and danced away with the ribbons of ballet shoes in their mouths. Araidne lost a pair of twins from her beginner's ballet class due to alleged cat-scratch fever; a major disaster as they had three younger sisters. She started to choreograph a ballet based on the kittens, but when Alfred opined that the adult human impersonating a cat was the most embarrassing sight in the universe, and the infant human doing so was only marginally better, she lost heart. Alfred received a deep scratch on his thumb while disentangling Tom from a curtain, infected it with paint, and had to wear a clumsy bandage, which made painting impossible. They hardly spoke, addressing most of their remarks to the kittens.

Then one grey day, while the taped carols of the Rotarians pierced the woolly hat he had pulled down over his ears to muffle them, sidestepping a plastic-suited Santa shaking a tin, Alfred Ellis entered the Craft Market, a portfolio in his good hand, shamefacedly and without hope, and found himself appreciated as an artist at last.

He sold several rough studies, executed sinisterly, of the kittens; posing under an umbrella, gazing up expectantly from a pair of old boots, entangled in a ball of knitting wool and needles, Tom asleep with his arms flung out behind his head and Beulah curled into him with her paws crossed, and was commissioned by a local gift shop to supply it with more, and was approached by three golden retrievers who wanted portraits of their owners, or vice versa.

It was almost midnight. The kittens lay in one another's arms; their new jewelled collars sending reflections of firelight and the broken baubles they had torn from the tree, which stood in a huge jagged hole in the wall, sparkling round the room as the last bong of Big Ben rang in the future; babies in rhinestones. And the parents? They stayed together for the sake of the children.